THE PROMISE

THE DRATH WAR

BOOK 1

MEYARI MCFARLAND

CONTENTS

SPECIAL OFFER

The rainbow has infinite shades, just as this collection covers the spectrum of fictional possibilities.

From contemporary romances like *The Shores of Twilight Bay* to dark fantasy like *A Lone Red Tree* and out to SF futures in *Child of Spring, Iridescent* covers the gamut of time, space and genre.

Meyari McFarland shows her mastery in this first omnibus collection of her short fiction. Twenty-five amazing stories, all with queer characters going on adventures, solving mysteries, and falling in love are here in the first Rainbow Collection.

And now you can get this massive collection of short queer fiction, all of it with the happy endings you love, *for free!*

Sign up here for your free copy of Iridescent now!

OTHER DRATH BOOKS BY MEYARI MCFARLAND:

Clash of Lines
Joining of Lines
Consort of the Crystal Palace
Fragments of a Chain
Stranded With You
Reunited Hearts
A Simple Life
Cradle of the Day

Also Available: The collected Drath Series:
The Drath Series Books 1-3
The Drath Series Books 4-6

You can find these and many other books at www.MDR-Publishing.com. Please sign up for our mailing list to get regular updates on the latest preorders and new releases and a free ebook!

Paperback ISBN: 978-1-64309-131-0

Hardback ISBN: 978-1-64309-211-9

Cover image:

Deposit Photo ID# **161302636** by TsuneoMP

Deposit Photo ID# **175800016** by agsandrew

This book is also available in TPB format from all major retailers.

❀ Created with Vellum

This story is dedicated to Dean Weasley Smith.

ONE
WITH AN OCEAN BREEZE

SALT FILLED the air as the sun dipped below the horizon, staining the ocean scarlet and gold as it went. The carefully gene-sculpted palms that stood along the waterline stood as perfect silhouettes against the glowing sky. The generation ship that had brought humanity here eight thousand years ago had done a good job spreading across this world. They'd colonized not just the various continents scattered across the northern hemisphere, but also the clusters of archipelagos that dotted the southern oceans.

Narcisse smiled as she leaned her elbows on the real wood of their table. Real wooden table, real wool stuffing the floor pillow she'd curled up on, and even real wooden mugs for the drinks she and her little sister Tracey had ordered when they arrived. Heck, there were real cooks in the kitchen at the back of the restaurant, talking to each other as they grilled fish and chopped mango, lime and the local version of spinach that was sweet-smelling instead of bitter.

The restaurant was small, just one big room built over top of a general store downstairs, but the food smelled delightful. Whoever had decorated the dining room, they'd had a great eye for color. Sarong decorated with embroidered geometric patterns and dyed flowers the size of Narcisse's head covered the walls. Big leafy plants arched over the four tables in the dining room, giving each table the impression that it alone had that perfect view out over the ocean towards the sunset.

The light breeze that had been so delightfully refreshing during the heat of the tropical day turned chilly enough that Narcisse drew her wrap up around her shoulders. Probably should have chosen a restaurant up the street with inside seating for dinner, but with the balcony's view out over the boardwalk and the ocean beyond, how could she resist?

This entire trip had seemed like a ridiculous idea when Tracey first proposed it, but now Narcisse had to admit that Tracey had had a point. Getting away from work and home and their ridiculous family and their obnoxious nosiness was well worth it.

Of course, getting away from their family took getting on a space liner, traveling halfway across the human sphere, and hiding away on a quiet little island in the middle of the biggest archipelago in the southern ocean instead of staying in the capital city or just taking a quiet break at home. Mum would've been over every single day to make sure that her girls were eating properly and keeping their claws properly trimmed.

"You can't risk anything when you work with chemicals," Mum always said, eyeing Narcisse's fingers as if her claws could be trimmed even further past the quick. "An acid up the sheath could cripple you."

Narcisse huffed and automatically studied her claws.

Still short, no polish or decorations. The hints of her claw points at the tips of her fingers were still stubby and rounded rather than razor sharp the way they were engineered to be. It honestly wasn't that much of a problem. Annoying not to be able to pick things up with just her claws the way Tracey did, but Mum wasn't wrong that sharp claws made for a big problem when you worked with chemicals.

Narcisse still rubbed at the tips of her fingers, wishing idly that she could let them get sharp again, no matter how stupid that would be on the job.

"You're thinking about Mum," Tracey announced as she slid in to the seat opposite Narcisse with a big grin.

Narcisse sighed and stopped rubbing her fingers together. "Did you see our order?"

"Nope," Tracey said even though that was why she'd left their table in the first place. "But I did see some very lovely people coming in. We're going to have company shortly."

"Really?" Narcisse asked with a frown that she tried to ease off her face before Tracey could complain about it.

Just because Tracey liked talking to people didn't mean Narcisse wanted to spend the whole evening listening to strangers gabbing at her. Not terribly fair of Narcisse. She'd had days and days of quiet and no people. One night with a few other people at the same restaurant wasn't going to hurt her.

Though that did depend on what sort of people Narcisse was going to have to cope with.

"Yep," Tracey said.

She grinned and then wagged her eyebrows without saying another word. Annoying girl. Narcisse opened her mouth to ask, justifiably harshly, who Tracey had seen but then it was a moot point because the other group came up the stairs in a little cluster.

Around a Drath.

Narcisse snapped her mouth shut.

A Drath. An old and cranky looking Drath who climbed the stairs like every paw raised upwards made her spine creak and her joints pop.

All the Drath looked fierce. It was hard for them not to when they were furry predators the size of a large pony or a small horse from Old Earth. Their muzzles and forward-facing eyes looked like a wolf's, though their ears were long like a rabbit's or a mule's and their skulls much broader. Same for the neck and shoulders and the haunches, which always made Narcisse think that the Drath's evolutionary ancestors were short-burst pursuit predators who'd been driven to hunt on savannas by a climate change that altered their environment dramatically enough that they evolved long legs to go along with their heavily muscled shoulders and haunches.

Powerful but long-legged, the Drath looked like animals.

Until you looked at the stubby fingers on all four paws.

Until you saw the long prehensile tail with its hand-like appendage at the end.

Until you stared them in the eyes.

Which Narcisse realized she was absolutely doing to the old, cranky, very sore and tired-looking Drath at the head of the stairs. Narcisse blushed and huffed at Tracey who was grinning at Narcisse with her chin on her hands and endless teasing clearly waiting on her tongue.

"You could've warned me!" Narcisse hissed at her.

"And miss you making googly eyes at the Drath?" Tracey said, giggling. "No way! Besides, I was much more focused on the Drath's companions."

"Who?" Narcisse blinked and then looked, going blazingly red that she'd somehow missed the three humans with the Drath.

Three very fit, very beautiful, very fierce-looking humans.

All three of which grinned at Tracey and Narcisse because the dining room was far too small for them not to have overheard every single word they'd said. Narcisse groaned and swatted Tracey who cackled at her before waving the group over.

"Might as well join us," Tracey said with a huge, welcoming grin. "I'm Tracey Hogan. This is my older sister Narcisse. We've put our orders in but only just. You could probably get orders in and have them arrive about the same time as ours if you hurry."

"I'll get that," the tallest of the three humans said, body abruptly shifting from muscular and masculine to equally muscular but busty with pronounced hips that gave their walk a very distracting sway as they headed back toward the kitchen to put in their group's dinner orders.

Oh.

Gensyn.

Huh.

For some reason, Narcisse hadn't expected that they would meet any Gensyn on this trip even though they were only one solar system away from the Gensyn system. No way were she and Tracey going to go to the Gensyn system. It was far too dangerous with all the solar flares, debris and raiders that the Gensyn didn't bother cleaning out.

While the Gensyn had used their genetic engineering and nanites to make themselves virtually indestructible and capable of shifting build from masculine to feminine and back at will, Narcisse and Tracey's ancestors had focused far more on making their children smart, fast and deadly enough to survive against the threats on their home world.

But even though the Gensyn were the most successful of the descendants of Old Earth, spread all over the human sphere by the Drath's gift of the FTL Wave Drive, Narcisse had just assumed that they wouldn't meet any.

Stupid of her.

"You don't mind?" the Drath asked as she slowly and very stiffly stalked over to the table.

Narcisse sighed. "No, not really. Tracey's the gabby one. I'll just listen and swat her from time to time when she gets too ridiculous."

Tracey stuck her tongue out at Narcisse, ducking the half-hearted swat that demanded from Narcisse. Rather than pay attention Tracey and give her the chance to tease even more, Narcisse got up and got several more floor cushions, laying them out so that the Drath could lay down somewhat comfortably. The cushions weren't quite large enough, but they were fluffy and there were plenty so that Narcisse could make a low couch of sorts for the old Drath to settle on.

At least the table was a low enough one that they would all be more or less at eye level.

"Close," the Drath commented as she carefully eased herself down onto the floor pillows and then sighed. "But not quite."

Her head ended up over twenty centimeters above Narcisse's. The Drath's powerful body was so thick with muscle that even reclining, it was like sitting next to a tank. Narcisse blinked and stared up at the Drath whose ears went floppy all of a sudden. Her mouth went loose, too, like a happy dog smiling at you, while the Drath's tail curled into corkscrew loops.

"What's so funny?" The shortest of the three human companions asked.

"Tall," Narcisse said, leaning around the Drath to stare wide-eyed at them.

The Drath laughed harder, shoulders and flanks shaking with silent laughter.

"Shani is tall," the shortest Gensyn agreed with a grin. "I'm Matija Planche. Payton Wu was the one who went to put our orders in. This is Chikere Applehof, our lead. We're Shani's escort while she's exploring the planet."

"I'm an anthropologist," Shani explained, ears still floppy and lips loose enough with amusement that Narcisse could see Shani's long fangs. "It's fascinating seeing how humanity has altered itself for the various worlds you've colonized."

"Really?" Narcisse said, tipping her head to the side more for a chance to watch Payton saunter back, hips swinging, than anything else. It was a lovely sight. "I would've thought that all the other races altered themselves to the worlds they colonized. Or did they change the worlds to match themselves?"

Shani's lips tightened back up as she turned to stare down at Narcisse. It was a forbidding sort of stare. Between Shani's long muzzle that hid long, sharp meat-cutting teeth, and the thunderously furry eyebrows that beetled over her golden hourglass pupil eyes, Shani's stare was ferocious enough to make Narcisse's stomach clench.

But Shani's nose twitched as she sniffed at Narcisse as curiously as Narcisse watched the minute movements of her eyes, the way her pupils expanded and contracted along with the snuffling of her nose, and the little tremors of the fur across Shani's shoulders.

She was curious. Perhaps as curious as Narcisse was.

"Don't get your head bitten off," Tracey said as she swatted Narcisse's shoulder.

"No, no biting, I don't think," Narcisse said thoughtfully. "Your nose is your primary sense, isn't it? Our noses are better than most humans but we're still primarily visual. I haven't quite… gotten a handle on your scent yet."

"Mm, agreed," Tracey said, chin on her folded hands. Her eyes were mostly shut despite the frowns on Matija, Payton and Chikere's faces. "Sort of spicy? There's a bit of musk but I can't tell what that means. Or if it's just, you know, background scent of Drath."

Shani turned and stared at Tracey, sniffing at her just as intensely as she'd sniffed at Narcisse. "You're more altered than I thought."

Narcisse shrugged. "Our world is fairly dangerous, actually. We have sub-dermal armor, claws with venom, fangs with venom and heightened senses of smell. Not dramatically. We're not Dragons, of course, but we can scent a good bit more than a Baseline human from Old Earth could."

The spicy scent slowly seeping up off of Shani's fur stayed steady, but the musky scent abruptly increased. Narcisse fought the urge to grin. Curiosity. Musk was curiosity. It was a nice sort of musk, not to thick and rank that it made you choke.

Interestingly, all three of the Gensyn scowled at Narcisse and Tracey as if they'd suddenly declared their intent to attack Shani. Narcisse turned her attention to them instead, studying them to see what exactly they'd decided made two civilians so threatening.

Other than claws with venom, of course. People always overreacted to that.

Matija's dark cheeks went brick red as she met Narcisse's eyes squarely. She raised her chin like she wanted to fight. Chikere put one hand on the blaster on her hip as she glowered at Narcisse with ice-blue eyes that were nearly neon against the burnished bronze of her hair and skin. The only one who didn't look immediately threatening was Payton, and that was only because Payton's night-black, perfectly oval face betrayed no emotion at all.

"It's the venom, right?" Narcisse asked. None of the Gensyn responded, but Shani started laughing again. "Goodness, everyone always makes such a fuss over that. You're Gensyn. You heal too quickly for us to really harm you. A fish, an animal, or an unaltered human, sure, we could affect them with the venom. Possibly Shani but I understood that you have nanites in your bloodstream that are even more advanced that the Gensyn's?"

Shani laughed harder, head dipping until her nose nearly brushed against the wooden table. "Oh, goodness, I do love humans. Yes, child, we do have nanites. You're nowhere near lethal enough to hurt me. Or them."

"Exactly," Narcisse said. "I mean, I'm ninety-eight percent harmless.

My claws are blunt. Tracey might be able to scratch you, but I couldn't do even that."

"Who clipped your claws?" Shani asked, all laughter disappeared into another thunderous scowl that matched perfectly to the rumbling growl sounding through Shani's chest.

"...Now I'm really wondering exactly how you vocalize," Narcisse said, staring at Shani's chest. "That's fascinating. I don't suppose I can climb all over you and feel exactly where the growls and vocalizations come from, can I?"

Tracey groaned and swatted Narcisse's shoulder again. "She's a chemist. She trimmed her claws herself so that she wouldn't get any acids up in the claw sheathe."

"It's horribly painful, potentially disfiguring and always embarrassing when that happens," Narcisse said.

Her fingers twitched to massage Shani's muscular body. Terribly rude idea but goodness, how did Drath vocalizations work, anyway? Jaw like that, teeth like a predator's. They shouldn't be able to make sounds at all like a human's and yet Shani's voice sounded like a particularly deep human voice, not like anything alien. If she'd heard Shani recorded, she wouldn't have realized that Shani was a Drath until she growled.

Possibly not even then.

"You're definitely a scientist," Shani said. She shifted around and flopped onto her side, putting her head in Narcisse's lap. "Go right ahead. And if you feel any tight muscles, feel free to use those clever fingers your people have to loosen them up."

Narcisse beamed. "Thank you, I will!"

"Oh Gods," Tracey groaned and laughed while shaking her head. "I can't believe you. It never fails. Something fuzzy shows up and it's in your lap in minutes. My sister. You're so ridiculous."

True enough that Narcisse pretended that she hadn't heard a word of it. Let Tracey chat with the Gensyn. Narcisse was absolutely more interested in running her fingers through Shani's wonderful fur, seeking out her skin under the long outer coat's dark layers, the inner coat's thick light-tan down.

There were a lot of tense muscles on Shani's scalp. Even more on her short, powerful neck. Those shoulders were a mess of knotted muscles. Narcisse smiled and set to work massaging as much as she could loose before dinner arrived.

Why not? She'd been given permission, and it was always going to be better to help someone relax than it was to attempt to talk and flirt, especially when she got to help an old Drath feel better. Who know? It might lead to interesting discussions and scientific revelations later on.

TWO
AROUND A STURDY TABLE

THERE WAS something distinctly Altered about Narcisse and Tracey. Payton wasn't used to encountering other humans who were Altered and yet not visibly different. Well, Gensyn were visibly different, in that they could shift, but their real Alterations had been in their durability. Not many species of humanity could come close to the durability of a Gensyn.

Payton rather wondered just how much Narcisse could survive. She and her sister seemed to be sweet, gentle, harmless, even. Until Tracey curled her claws out of the tips of her fingers and left an etched mark against the side of her glass.

"What?" Tracey asked, eyes wide as Payton stiffened and Matija's eyes went wide.

"Mug," Narcisse said even though she'd seemed to be fully involved with petting, skritching and generally flopping all over Shani who looked as though she might never, ever move again having been rendered into a puddle of happy Drath.

"What?" Tracey asked, with more confusion. She looked at her glass and turned bright red. "Oh, damn. I always forget not to fidget with these things. They're so fragile."

"Just how sharp are your claws?" Payton asked and didn't feel the need to apologize for the snap in xyr voice.

"Eh, not that sharp," Tracey complained as she tried to polish the mark out with her sleeve and then groaned because, obviously, that wasn't going to work. "I mean, they're sharp, yeah, but not like they should be. I haven't even been sharpening them."

"They naturally go to a very fine point," Narcisse explained while running her fingers through Shani's fur and grinning at the way Shani groan-growled in pleasure. "It's not so much that our claws are terribly sharp. It's the way the keratin at the tip is shaped and the venom sting's interaction with it."

"True," Tracey said, nodding towards Narcisse while staring over Payton's shoulder. "The sting's really sharp, like monomolecular fine point. It's part of how we deliver venom into attacking critter's bodies. Tiny little needle-like tip delivering really nasty venom and yay, we don't die!"

Payton didn't laugh. Xe couldn't find their calmness about being so lethal amusing, even if Chikere and Matija snickered over it. At very least, Chikere should take it seriously. Narcisse was all over Shani, and it was their job to keep Shani safe until she recovered properly.

"Tracey's claws are sharp," Narcisse said with a little flick of a glance that might be a weak apology towards Payton. "Mine aren't. Our mum insists that I dull my claws practically daily."

"And she resents it bitterly but refuses to say a word about it," Tracey added with a roll of her eyes that was fond rather than scornful.

"That's a blatant lie," Narcisse replied, shifting to rubbing Shani's shoulders and smiling with innocent joy as Shani groaned happily.

Tracey all but speared her sister with a stern glower that Narcisse paid no attention to at all. Not that Payton could believe that Narcisse was unaware. The stiffness of her shoulders and the jutting set of her jaw said that she was quite aware of Tracey's glare and refused to acknowledge it.

Possibly for older sibling knows best reasons.

Or maybe "I'm not going to pick that fight with our parent so go knock yourself out with a grenade" reasons. Payton's eyes slid to Chikere who smiled at the two of them just like a parent who was amused by their antics but wasn't going to say it lest xe encouraged their behavior.

"Children," Chikere drawled, proving Payton's point with a lazy little smirk at the two of them. "No fighting at the table."

"We're not fighting," Tracey said, arms crossed defiantly over her chest as she stared out over the sea.

Narcisse snorted and didn't so much as look over her shoulder at Chikere. "Don't even try the Mum voice on me, ma'am. You're not going to match our actual mum's tone. Your voice is far too low for that to work."

Chikere swallowed a startled laugh while Payton stared at Narcisse. "Well, that's not a reaction I'm used to. What world did you two say you come from?"

"We didn't," Narcisse said with a quicksilver grin that was wild enough to make Payton's heart thump in xyr chest.

It wasn't the smile, so much. Narcisse's smile was just a smile. What made xyr heart lurch was the sudden flash of danger in her eyes, in the way she curled her lip just so, exposing the tip of a fang. A venomous fang, no less.

Sweet, kind, gentle, terrifyingly smart and… lethal.

Damn it, Payton really had a type. One that knocked xem off-balance at the most inconvenient times.

"Why do you need to know?" Tracey asked in much the same "dare you to push it" tone.

"…Is that somehow making a threat?" Payton asked as Matija edged closer to xem without interfering in Payton or Matija's aim if Narcisse or Tracey attacked.

Narcisse snorted a laugh, fingers still busy petting Shani who was so utterly relaxed that Payton wanted to check Shani's pulse. Again. Damn it, Shani had better not be having a relapse. They still had to get off this island and back to the mainland where the rest of her pack was dealing with the local's idiotic politics.

"No, but if you're going to treat us like we're a threat, why shouldn't we act like one?" Narcisse said far too reasonably. "Stop being so stiff, silly. Dinner is almost ready, and this fluffy enormous lady needs to wake up before my legs fall asleep."

"No waking," Shani mumbled without moving her jaw at all. "Only petting."

"Really, how do you talk?" Narcisse asked with so much fascination that Payton wanted to yell at her. "That wasn't with your throat or your mouth."

"It really wasn't, was it?" Tracey asked as she leaned over the sturdy wooden table to stare at Shani with equal fascination. "Do you know why they're so freaked out, Shani? It's kind of um, unfortunate."

Shani opened one eye and then flipped an ear that almost hit Narcisse in the face. "I'm kind of sick, actually. Got hit with some… toxins… that hurt my sinuses and inflamed most every joint I have. My pod's off on the mainland and I'm here alone so I don't have a proper first aid kit to deal with it."

"And our communications were cut off," Matija complained.

Payton glowered at xer. "That's need-to-know information, Matija."

"Sorry," Matija muttered though xe didn't look all that sorry about it at all.

Narcisse frowned.

Not at Payton, Chikere or Matija as Tracey did. No, Narcisse frowned down at Shani with so much worry that Payton nearly rolled xyr eyes at the sheer ridiculousness. The next moment, Narcisse started carefully working her hands over Shani's shoulders, elbows and hips, grunting and muttering incoherently under her breath.

"That swollen?" Tracey asked.

"Yeah," Narcisse said, still frowning. "I'd bet that your joints are twice the size they should be. Shouldn't you be getting evacuated out? This feels like a medical emergency, which is definitely not time to stop for dinner."

Shani snorted, her tail going into a tight corkscrew. "Oh, we sent a message to my pack. Drath nanites are better then Gensyn nanites, though, so they're not likely to worry. Frankly, food will do me more good than anything else. Nanites do need fuel, you know."

Surprisingly, Narcisse didn't relax when Tracey did. She stiffened and stared at Shani so sternly that Payton's spine stiffened and xyr hand dropped down to xyr blaster at the same time that Payton cataloged every add-on component that would transform xyr blaster from mid-range into lethal sniper-worthy. Shani opened both eyes to stare up at Narcisse with her ears back in what looked like astonishment. The corkscrew of her tail relaxed utterly and her starfish-like tail-hand brushed over Shani's ankles nervously.

"You've got nanites that are better than Gensyn nanites," Narcisse said slowly, too slowly, "and yet you're not healing?"

That was… Payton shifted on xyr floor pillow, eyebrows going up at the sheer power of the Mom-voice Narcisse used. Shani squirmed uncomfortably, stubby finger-toes tapping against the floor and tail-hand waving aimlessly before Shani sighed.

"That's actually a good point," Tracey said just as slowly but with a worried expression and tone. "I mean, it must have been a terrible toxin to hit you that hard."

"Targeted to me," Shani admitted.

Narcisse sucked in a sharp breath, nodding towards the kitchen while frowning at Tracey. "Go see if dinner is ready. That's worrisome."

"Extremely," Tracey agreed. "You three stay here. Your noses aren't good enough to tell if someone spiked the food. Ours are."

"You will stay right here," Narcisse scolded Shani when she kicked a leg as if she was going to get up and follow Tracey to the kitchen. "You're the target, silly. You don't go haring off putting yourself in danger. That's ridiculous."

Payton huffed and went to follow Tracey to the kitchen. She turned and glowered at xem, claws flexing out dramatically, so Payton froze and slowly sat back down. Tracey nodded firmly and trotted off to the kitchen. A moment later, she started chatting cheerfully and loudly with the kitchen staff, asking what everything was and generally making a pest of herself.

When xe'd gone back to the kitchen, Payton had been very firmly escorted to the door by the scowling head chef. Xe had tried to protest, had tried to say that xe needed to verify the food, but the head chef, a burly woman with a cleaver as long as Payton's thigh and thick enough to be able to go through xyr femur with a single swipe, wouldn't hear of it.

Tracey giggled and soon had the whole kitchen giggling with her.

"Tracey's good at people," Narcisse said with a little nodded apology and a wry smile. She'd obviously seen Payton's surprise. "I don't blame you for being offended by it. Sometimes it seems like the entire universe is full of people that are brand new life-long friends that Tracey just hasn't met yet."

"Not you?" Shani asked. A moment later, Shani's ribs shook with silent laughter and her tail went into the tightest corkscrew belly laugh that Payton had seen yet.

"Only if it's someone with fur I can pet," Narcisse said, giggling and petting Shani some more. "I'm not much of a people person."

"I have food!" Tracey declared, startling Payton into whirling and nearly smashing xyr head into the heavy serving tray she was carrying. "Whoops, you almost got to wear dinner, there. It's all lovely. I think you'll like it, Shani. I got them to combine our order with you guys' order. There's a little bit of everything."

Tracey set the tray down as Narcisse helped Shani roll back onto her belly. The two of them seemed so very harmless. And then so dangerous when Tracey curled her claws out around a bowl of fish that had been chopped into thumb-sized chunks. Shani's ears went back against her skull, disappearing into her ruff.

Poisoned.

Narcisse casually set that bowl aside, off at the end of the table out of everyone's reach. She snagged a little bowl full of chopped green and red fruit of some sort, adding it to the end of the table. Once they were out of the way, they served everyone, chatting companionably with Shani about the fish they'd eaten so far, and with Matija and Chikere about the other foods they'd had while on vacation.

They could detect poisons. They could fight. They had sub-dermal armor apparently, and noses that compared favorably with the Drath.

Shani trusted them.

Payton glanced at Matija, wondering if xe thought as Payton did. They needed allies if they were going to get Shani back to her people without getting all of them killed. Xe didn't want to involve civilians, but allowing the Drath under their care, allowing Shani in particular, to be killed would mean the Drath would destroy everyone.

Everyone on this planet.

All the Gensyn.

Perhaps all of humanity.

Shani sighed and refused to meet Payton's eyes. Xe bit xyr lip and set to work eating as quickly as possible. They had to get Shani to her people. If it took conscripting Tracey and Shani, so be it. Hopefully, Tracey and Shani would agree to help. They certainly weren't going to make it otherwise.

THREE
WITH A SLOW STRIDE

SOMEONE EARNESTLY WANTED SHANI DEAD. The toxin in the fish and the pico de gallo was a nasty little thing. She wasn't familiar with the particular form of it, but it was a combination of several heavy metals, something that smelled rather like tetrodotoxin and a masking fluid that might, possibly, be nanite-enhanced.

Dangerous and quite horrific, either way. The nanite portion seemed quite certain. When Tracey had delivered the food to the table, the metallic scent of the toxin had been quite faint. By the time they were all happily eating their way through some delicious ice cream and a shared mango and peach tart that was the most amazing thing to ever have been in Narcisse's mouth, the fish and the pico de gallo stank of the toxin.

Tracey glanced at it; cheeks rather too pale.

Narcisse nodded once, utterly agreeing with Tracey's terrified desire to get those two dishes somewhere off the table. "I'll be right back."

"Don't you dare," Shani murmured. "They'll know."

"Oh, they already know that you caught the toxin," Narcisse said, nodding towards the kitchen where one of the kitchen staff members kept peeking out and then looking like he was about to be gutted. "I just want to flush those. Can't let anyone ever eat from those again. The toxin will soak into the wood and contaminate—"

Narcisse squeaked as Payton pulled xyr blaster and blew the end of the table off.

It did, also, neatly deal with the problem of how to dispose of the tainted fish and pico de gallo, but seriously! Narcisse huffed at xem, rolling her eyes when Payton just grimly nodded as if that was a perfectly logical way to handle the problem.

"You're paying for that table," Narcisse declared, wagging a finger at Payton.

"I—" Payton immediately started to protest. Xe snapped xyr mouth shut as Tracey and Narcisse both glared at xem.

"You're paying for it," Narcisse repeated. "Goodness, what a ridiculous way to handle a problem. There's a fireplace in the back of the restaurant. I was going to flush the contents and then toss the bowls in there. Much less noticeable."

Which would still have been quite obvious to the server, but now they had the manager hustling over with a thunderous scowl and Shani still smelled like she ached abominably. There hadn't been enough time for the food to help her heal up properly.

Military people. They were so used to dealing with threats that everything became a blow-it-up solution, even if that made it worse.

"Sorry," Narcisse said.

"Yeah," Tracey said, putting on her most earnestly apologetic expression. "It was an allergy thing and Payton overreacted. But xe'll totally pay for the table, right, Payton?"

Payton rubbed xyr forehead. "Fine. I'll pay for it. I won't apologize for keeping Shani alive, but I'll pay for the stupid table."

The manager, a fussy middle-aged woman whose sarong bunched unattractively around her hips huffed. Her expression was a perfect mask of outrage mixed with avarice, but that's all it was.

A mask.

Her scent was frustration. Denied her target. Urgent need to get to the back office and call for reinforcements.

Tracey's eyes widened just enough for Narcisse to confirm that she'd caught it, too. Then the two of them moved, leaping straight over their tablemates to tackle the manager to the floor. Tracey kept her claws in so that she didn't claw the manager to pieces.

Narcisse didn't bother.

It was generally a struggle to tailor ones' venom to the situation. There was no fast way to do it so most of their people left their venom at "kill a beastie but not a person" level. Since coming her on vacation, Tracey hadn't put in the meditation or effort to shift hers.

Narcisse had spent the entire dinner focusing on her venom and shifting it to instant knockout with rapid paralysis toxins.

The manager squawked as Narcisse punched her claws into her shoulder.

Then she collapsed limply to the floor, eyes rolling back and breathing slowly subsiding to a bare whisper in her chest.

"That's that," Narcisse said, shaking her fingertips. "She was part of the plot. We'd best go right away."

She turned back to Shani, Payton, Matija and Chikere. All of them stared at Narcisse. So did Tracey with a raised eyebrow and a little smirk. Narcisse huffed.

"Seriously, we'd best hurry or the people in the kitchen will call whoever it is that's stalking you," Narcisse said.

"I wondered what you were going for during dinner," Tracey said. "Nice choice."

"...What." Payton's voice came out so flat that it wasn't really a question, except that xyr expression absolutely made it a frantic one.

Narcisse shrugged. "We can adjust how our venom glands produce the venom. I worked during dinner to make a good knockout version. Let's go."

She went and helped Shani stand, massaging Shani's shoulders when her fore-legs nearly gave out underneath her. It was a little odd to have a Drath lean against her. Narcisse's chin could've rested on Shani's shoulder. If Shani was a bit healthier, Narcisse suspected that she'd be big enough and strong enough for Narcisse to ride her like a horse.

Not that Narcisse would dare.

That would be so very rude. You didn't ride people unless you were a tiny baby and your aunties or uncles volunteered. Narcisse hadn't dared to ask anyone for a ride since Tracey was born. That was for little kids and Narcisse had decided that she was a big kid as soon as she had a little sister.

It seemed like a distant pity as Narcisse helped Shani down the stairs with Payton guarding the rear with Tracey while Chikere and Matija went first, weapons at the ready. Outside, the wind had picked up to a good stiff breeze coming off the ocean. It blew all the scents of town away, leaving only the thick smell of sea salt mixing with the inevitable scent of shellfish that'd died over the day in the sand.

There would be no checking to see who was coming by scent now. Worse, night had fallen. Outside of the circles of light from the street lamps along the street, the town was pitch back. Narcisse frowned, one hand on Shani's shaking shoulder. This was not a good situation. They could be ambushed at any moment, and they wouldn't see or smell the attack before it began.

"We need to get away from here," Narcisse announced.

"We know that," Payton complained. Xe glowered as if stating the obvious was the worst insult they'd ever received.

"No, I mean, we need to get away from this spot right now," Narcisse said. "There's too much light and too much wind. We can't smell or see an attack coming. We need somewhere darker with gentler winds and that means either heading for the dock—"

"We'll never get there," Tracey said, shaking her head as she fidgeted nervously, claws and fangs out and ready. "That's the obvious choice."

"Or we need to go further into town," Narcisse finished as if Tracey hadn't interrupted. "Find a truck or something, get away from here, away from town, get some space around us so that we don't get picked off without warning."

Payton looked to Chikere who grimaced and then nodded. Both Chikere and Matija smelled like they'd prefer to go the opposite direction. It was a logical choice.

If you knew what was hunting you. How big it was and how deadly. They had no idea and so retreat was the only plan that made sense. Narcisse nodded for Tracey to take the lead, smiling as Tracey pulled off her sandals and tucked them into her back which she slung crosswise over her chest so that it wouldn't fall off.

"Claws on the toes, too," Shani commented, ears up and rotating as she listened for trouble, just like Narcisse who kept her head moving so that she might, possibly, get lucky and hear an attacker before they could strike.

"Of course," Narcisse said. "Do your best to run. I'll be at your side. The Gensyn can guard your rear."

"What about in front?" Chikere demanded with enough outrage that Narcisse rolled her eyes.

"Anyone in front of us that doesn't get Tracey first will be dead," Narcisse said. "She hasn't modified her venom like I have."

That shut all three of the Gensyn up, which got them moving out of the light and down an alley at long last. The wind scoured Tracey's scent away almost as soon as she laid it down, toes flexing and claws leaving scores in the sandy soil. It wasn't wet enough tonight for Tracey's scent to cling but that was all right.

Shani put her nose down and followed Tracey like a bloodhound.

Away from the boardwalk, the lights spilled yellowed pools of illumination every third or fourth block. Most of them flickered as if they were on the verge of blowing out, so there was even less light than one would expect.

It was such a relief.

As soon as they stepped out of the yellow streetlights range, Narcisse's eyes adapted to the dark. Tropical palms bioengineered out of samples brought from Old Earth thrust spikey yellow-green leaves up towards the star-filled sky. To Narcisse's night vision, the yellow was dove grey. The green looked near-black.

Tracey's footsteps glowed faintly red in the darkness, showing her path.

She'd run ahead, doubled back, checked under the tropical shrub with the head-sized white flowers that shivered on the night breeze. Their scent was thick enough to choke Narcisse's nose, yet it mingled with the sand and the scent of salt to create a sort of background fabric to the night air that only pointed out the disruptions that much more clearly.

Tracey had rubbed the white flower's pollen all over her face and hands and shirt.

"Good," Narcisse murmured to Shani who limped along next to her, shoulder shaking under Narcisse's hand.

"Camouflaged her scent," Shani agreed. "Smart."

"Basic," Narcisse said, "but yes. Can you handle that?"

"No, it'd knock my nose right out of commission," Shani said. "If I was back to normal it'd be fine, but not now."

Narcisse nodded. "I am very, very unhappy with how slowly you're healing."

Shani snort-laughed as her ears went floppy and her tail curled into a corkscrew. "You and me both."

Three blocks from the boardwalk, Tracey stopped doubling back and checking everything. She started checking for vehicles of any sort that'd been left open. Her heat trail and scent marked every single truck, sled and flyer along the sandy road.

Then her scent went onwards into the darker streets further away from the boardwalk. The engineers of the town had apparently decided that there was no point to putting streetlights up away from the boardwalk. While Narcisse had seen them scattered along the back streets parallel to the ocean, as they went further and further from the boardwalk, fewer lights existed.

In six blocks the only lights came from individual houses where flying insects battered themselves against the bulbs and from the stars overhead. The wind dyed down as well, finally letting the scents laying across the land a chance to settle.

"Ah," Narcisse breathed as she leaned close to Shani's neck. "I smell them now."

"You do?" Shani asked, ears flicking forward, back, forward, back as she searched for what Narcisse had picked up on.

"Mm," Narcisse agreed. "They're off to the left, to the east. They patrolled through here a few hours ago. It's the smell of their weapons. Chemical-based as well as standard blasters. I ah, helped engineer the oil they used to clean the blasters. Recently, that is."

"Huh," Shani grunted. "Any idea how many?"

Narcisse shut her eyes and breathed deep, trying to sift the old smells of the patrolling warriors, whoever they were, out of the scents of all the locals who'd come through since then. It wasn't easy. The hair started to go up on the back of her neck because it almost smelled like the warriors had gone door to door, like they'd talked to everyone in town.

Other than Narcisse and Tracey, two silly tourist girls from off-world who clearly weren't a threat or interesting at all.

"Everyone in town is a threat," Narcisse whispered to Shani, well aware that her claws were digging into Shani's fur far too deeply. "I think they got all the town folk on their side for this... whatever it is."

Shani's ears snapped back against her skull as her tail went rigid behind her.

"What?" Payton asked just a hair too loudly for Narcisse's comfort.

"Assume everyone in town is a potential threat," Narcisse said. She looked into the darkness and then pulled off her shoes. "I'm going to get Tracey. Keep heading out of town. Go straight ahead of you. Don't stop and don't slow down. We'll catch up to you."

Payton opened xyr mouth to ask but Narcisse didn't stay to listen. She dug her toes in and ran into the darkness, intent on finding Tracey, on getting some sort of transport and then getting back to Shani as quickly as she could.

It was a little bit crazy to risk so much for an alien that Narcisse had only just met, but Narcisse couldn't imagine doing anything else. Shani needed help. She was funny and wonderful and beautiful. Narcisse's instincts said to help, so she would help.

And let the Gods defend anyone who got in Narcisse's way because Narcisse would give them no mercy.

FOUR
AGAINST A SURPRISE THREAT

"WAIT!" Payton hissed, not that it did a damn bit of good as Narcisse dashed off into the darkness, leaving them to defend Shani by themselves.

Narcisse disappeared into the darkness like a ghost. Payton's heart rate immediately picked up. Dramatically. How could it not? They were in much more danger now that Narcisse and Tracey had left them alone in the flower-scented night.

Which should be nuts given that Payton, Chikere and Matija had weapons. Narcisse and Tracey only had the claws and fangs they'd been born with. If anything, they should be in danger and Payton should feel safer with them away from here.

Xe didn't. Exact opposite, actually.

It said a lot that xe did consider the situation much more deadly without Narcisse and Tracey there. Two outright civilians who they'd met by pure accident were the best chance they had of keeping Shani safe.

This entire job was cursed. Xe'd known from the outset that this was a bad idea. Next time. Next time, xe wasn't going to ignore xyr instincts, especially when they screamed this loudly.

"What the hell?" Matija asked, eyes on the darkness that none of them could really see through. "Where'd she run off to? Why?"

"She's getting her sister and transport for us," Shani explained. "Your noses couldn't keep up with the conversation. Sorry."

She paced along entirely too calmly for the deadly situation. Yes, Shani's ears rotated constantly, and her nose twitched as she tried to catch scents of whoever was behind this. If it was Payton, xe would've been at least jogging. Xyr heart was absolutely pounding against xyr breastbone as xe paced Shani, weapon at the ready.

The night was far too dark. Xe understood Narcisse's insistence that they get away from the town's streetlights but xe really hated that xe couldn't see what was going on off in the shadows. There was damned little on this planet that could permanently damage Payton, Chikere, and Matija. There wasn't much in the universe that could take a Gensyn down for good. Most of it would have blown the entire island off the planet's surface and changed its global weather patterns for a good century or two.

No one was stupid or desperate enough to unleash that sort of firepower.

Shani, on the other hand, was terrifyingly vulnerable right now. It wasn't supposed to be this way. Shani should be even more indestructible than Payton was. Her superiors had more or less scoffed at the idea of anything on-world being able to hurt her. The curled lips, exposed fangs, and unamused snorts Payton had gotten at the suggestion that they might want to invest in more protection for Shani than just three Gensyn guards had been... well. Payton hadn't pissed xyr pants, but it'd been a close thing when the oldest Drath snapped at xyr head.

Showed what they knew.

All day long, there'd been birds. Critters of some sort had chattered in the shrubbery. People talking, moving around, machines running. Xe had spent the entire day jumping at random noises, waiting for the attack to come.

Now the night was dead silent other than their footsteps along the sandy road. Payton's heart beat in xyr ears was louder than anything else, to the point that xyr stomach churned acid up the back of xyr throat. Xe glowered into the night, ears straining and eyes squinting for any kind of warning for the coming attack.

Xe didn't need to see it to know that it was coming.

Soon.

The only warning Payton got was a faint whine through the air like a flying insect before xe took a needle to the face.

One second xe was peering around one of the spikey bushes covered with white flowers that seemed so popular here. The next xyr whole head whipped around, agony blooming. Payton was on the sandy street before xe realized that xe'd been shot.

"Down!" Chikere shouted at Shani.

Shani dropped, tail-hand firm against Payton's back to keep xem from rolling straight back to xyr feet.

A good idea.

Xyr jaw hung loose on the left side. Payton's breath caught in xyr chest as xe shoved xyr jaw back into place and smoothed xyr flesh back where it should be. The needle had been a big one. It took a solid eight seconds, far too long, for Payton's flesh to knit back together, for the tendons to reattach and the skin to scab over.

Not much blood, just enough to wash the sand out of the wound before the flesh sealed up again. Payton spat out the sand-filled blood clogging the back of xyr throat and then shoved upwards despite Shani's tail-hand trying to restrain xem.

"Where?" Payton snapped, voice hoarse and hands shaking.

"Everywhere," Shani replied.

Her tail-hand caught Payton, keeping xem from charging off into the darkness to clear a path out of there. Payton snarled at her. They needed to get away! Now!

"No," Shani replied, entirely calmly. "We need to hold until Narcisse and Tracey get back."

As soon as Shani spoke, the night lit up with blaster fire over their heads. Blasters and needlers, a few chemical guns that flung lead pellets like something out of an Old Earth drama, too. Payton hunched over Shani's back, grateful that she'd put her head right down to the sand and flattened her body so much that she seemed only ten or so centimeters thick.

Payton shuddered and tucked xyr face, injured side against Shani's soft fur, into the hollow between Shani's neck and her right foreleg. Xe bit xyr lip and tried to count the blasts, hoping without much hope that their attackers had cheap battery packs. If so, they'd get a dozen or so shots before they had to switch batteries.

No such luck.

The barrage of blaster fire seemed to be coming from behind the low stone walls that surrounded the yards of all the houses in the area. Payton didn't hear a single person stop to change packs which meant that they had professional-grade blasters. And, presumably profession-level assassination skills.

The white-flowered bush that loomed over them lost sprays of flower petals and showers of chopped leaves as their attackers blasted away at it as if to mow it down far enough that they could see Shani and kill her without exposing themselves to Payton, Chikere and Matija's weapons.

Oh.

That was what they were doing.

Payton narrowed xyr eyes as xe tracked the trajectories of the enemies destroying Shani's cover. Three quick blasts to the left over top of Shani's muscular back took out one party. Fewer than xe expected from the amount of fire. One shot in the other direction with Payton's blaster took care of the other set, or at least sent them scrambling so that they could get to a better, more defensible station.

"Chikere, take point!" Payton barked.

Silence met xem.

Xe turned and nearly started screaming as xe saw that Payton was alone in the street with Shani. Chikere was gone, tracks leading off down the street that ran west, parallel to the ocean's curving shore. Matija's tracks led straight back the way they'd come.

"They ran?" Payton hissed to Shani.

"Yeah," Shani said with a tired little sigh. "They never did really want this job. They don't like Drath all that much."

Payton stared at her as a muddle of emotions battled each other at the base of xyr throat. Anger, dismay, horror, embarrassment and finally outright offended pride that they would put their personal feelings ahead of the job. When they got back, not if because Payton was not going to fail, xe was going to report both of them for dereliction of duty to the guild.

If xe could, xe'd get them both fined as much as possible for this... behavior.

Distantly, the sarcastic voice that lived at the back of Payton's head that sounded like xyr terrible first lover cackled that Payton thought that xe would survive. And that xe thought a complaint like that would do any good.

"We have to move," Payton said, firing a few more shots towards the yard where the survivors cursed and shifted around behind the bushes.

"Will Narcisse be able to find us again?" Shani said with a short nod as her haunches bunched for a run.

"I doubt she'll have any problems," Payton said with a snort of bitter amusement. "She just has to follow the sound of the battle."

Shani's tail abruptly went into corkscrew loops. "True. Straight at them, through the yard and then onwards. More are coming towards our position."

"Go," Payton ordered.

And then had to scramble because when a Drath went, they *went*.

Shani leaped from her belly straight over the low stone fence, into the yard and then overtop of the attackers there. From the sudden smell of blood, she gutted at least one of them. Payton went over the wall, too, shooting one of the attackers in the face. The other swung at xem with a knife that Payton ignored as harmless. That one took a blast straight to the face. Their head went away in an explosion of bloody smoke, leaving Payton to run after Shani.

No lights, no allies, nothing to hide behind or use as shelter, damn it all. Shani wasn't running fast. In fact, she slowed down dramatically as soon as Payton spotted her ahead. Xe snarled at her, waving for her to run already.

"Not without you," Shani said, just a bit breathless which absolutely should not be for a predator with legs that came all the way up to Payton's waist.

"Will you move?" Payton snarled at her, shoving her onwards and then flinching when Shani almost fell over from xyr shove. "Damn it, why aren't you healing?"

"I wish I knew," Shani replied.

She gasped for air, nodded once and did her best to run. It was a good solid pace for Payton, a near-spring, but for Shani it was a stumbling shamble of a run. The further she went, the more she wheezed for breath. They barely made it to the edge of town where the big four-lane road ran around the perimeter of the island before she had to stop and brace all four legs to keep from collapsing on the spot.

Shani's head sagged to the dry, bone-white grass. "Can't."

"I know," Payton snarled as xe scanned the darkness. "How many? Can you tell?"

"Dozens," Shani wheezed. "Getting closer. I don't... can't..."

"Into the shrubs," Payton ordered because what else could xe do? "We'll hide. It won't work. They'll attack try to blow the shrubs up. That'll draw Narcisse and Tracey's attention."

Shani nodded and shuffled off the far side of the road where the extravagant flowering bushes were the size of mid-sized flyers instead of large shrubs like they were in town. The smell of the flowers was overwhelming for Payton's nose. Xe had no idea how Shani handled it, but she didn't make a single sound of protest as she crawled into the center of one of the huge shrubs, hiding behind a boulder that'd been consumed by the mass of flowers and spikey leaves.

Actually, there were six or so boulders arranged in a rough "U" which let Payton breathe for the first time all day. That was defensible. Not for long and not well, but it was better than anything they'd found so far.

Maybe, just maybe, they'd survive long enough for Narcisse to come back with some sort of help.

FIVE
WITH A DEADLY BREEZE

NARCISSE RACED THROUGH THE NIGHT, following Tracey's scent. Her heart raced as fear for Shani pounded in her blood. They had to get back to Shani right away. This was too dangerous. Shani was sick. Hurt, even.

It was... odd... that Narcisse was already so focused on Shani and her safety. The need to protect her was strong enough that Narcisse pushed the clinical portion of her mind to the rear so that she could focus on what mattered.

Find Tracey. Get transport. Get Shani somewhere safe. And Payton. Chikere and Matija, too, if they weren't too wishy-washy about protecting Shani.

Tracey'd run right past the edge of town and off into one of the machine shops along the tourist road that ran around the island. The place she'd chosen smelled of engine oil and fuel which made Narcisse grin with pride. That was her sister, making bright choices. Now hopefully she would have found—

Blaster fire exploded behind Narcisse.

"Shit!" Tracey shouted from one of the garages.

"What do you need?" Narcisse shouted back at her, running for all she was worth even though her feet skidded on the pavement and then dug in again on the sandy street on the far side of the road.

"Keys!" Tracey yelled back.

"Hijack it." Narcisse flailed her arms as she overshot the garage Tracey was in.

Her feet went out from under her, dropping Narcisse onto the ground. She flung out one hand, claws extended instinctively and then flinched a gasp as her thumb's claw shattered on impact with a buried rock. The queasy pain of the claw breaking off made sweat break out all over Narcisse's body, but she shoved herself back to her feet, panting, and then rushed into the shop where Tracey was waist-deep into the engine of an eight-person transport with lovely double doors on the back and what looked like decent armor on the top and sides.

"It's not working," Tracey complained only to gasp as the engine vibrated into life. She emerged from the engine with a huge grin. "Got it!"

"Good, hurry!" Narcisse ordered even though she wasn't quite sure if she would be able to keep that lovely dinner down until the claw grew back.

Tracey glanced at Narcisse with a worried frown, scent full of worry for the scent of Narcisse's pain, but neither of them slowed down enough to ask. Not when there was a pitched battle going on in town. Narcisse showed her rapidly healing claw with a grimace that Tracey matched.

Broken claws were so awful. It was why Narcisse hadn't bothered to work to sharpen her claws while they were on vacation. The slow way involved careful filing over the course of a few weeks. Tedious and not worth it when Narcisse would be back at work by the time she got them sharp.

The fast way involved breaking them off or straight-out cutting them off and letting them regrow.

No one sane did that, not unless they absolutely had to. Narcisse was worried enough about Shani that she wished she had a knife to chop all her claws off. She'd probably throw up and pass out if she did it. Not a good plan right now.

"Restraints," Tracey snapped as she buckled up.

"Just go already!" Narcisse huffed at her as she scrambled to get her restraints locked in without using her thumb.

Awkward but not impossible. Tracey, bless her heart, waited until Narcisse was buckled up before she gunned the engine and sped out of the garage. Someone, tomorrow, would be very upset about the missing van. Narcisse didn't care.

Not when blaster fire lit up the night and the whine of needlers pitching deadly projectiles through the darkness filled the air. Apparently, Shani and the Gensyn hadn't stayed where they'd been because the battle was a kilometer or so up the road from the garage. Narcisse squinted against the brightness of the battle, trying to figure out where Shani had to be hiding.

"Bushes?" Narcisse suggested.

"Probably," Tracey said, squinting just as hard. She shook her head. "Right, well, I'm going to fishtail it in there. Get the doors."

Thank all the Gods, there was a button on the dash for opening the big double doors without leaving your seat. Narcisse desperately wanted to be there at the door to help Shani, to pull her up into the transport and pet her to make sure she was all right.

There was no time for that nonsense.

Tracey flipped on the lights just before they reached the edge of the battle. The sudden blaze of light revealed about twenty people dressed in all-black with glasses over their eyes that had to be night vision goggles. Both Narcisse and Tracey grinned as the attackers flinched.

Then Tracey spun the wheel and Narcisse triggered the back doors to fling themselves open.

"Get in!" Narcisse yelled to Shani and the Gensyn.

Shani leaped up out of a shattered stack of smoking shrubbery, going up in a graceful leap that nearly ended in her smacking face-first into the sand when her front legs collapsed on landing. Payton dashed out with her, shoving xyr shoulder against Shani and keeping her upright just long enough for the two of them to tumble-roll into the back of the van.

"Go!" Payton bellowed.

Xe fired out of the back of the van at the attackers who were already turning and bringing their weapons back to bear.

"The others?" Tracey gasped as Narcisse slapped her hand against the door button.

"Gone," Shani replied with a wheeze that had Narcisse twisting around to reach out and touch her furry cheek. "Abandoned us. Go."

Tracey went.

The doors shut on Payton's barrage of blaster fire. Xe left one scorch mark on the inside while the attackers left dozens on the rear end of the transport. Narcisse's heart pounded so hard that she couldn't hear Payton's cursing clearly.

The armor on the transport held.

Tracey accelerated, flinging them at top speed away from the attackers. She turned off all the running lights, the headlights, even the lights in the cab so that they would be a fast-moving dark blur against the darkness of the night.

"They'll bring in flyers," Narcisse warned.

"I know, I know," Tracey said. "They've got to have trackers on you guys. Not us, probably, but certainly on the two of you."

"I would've smelled it," Shani protested.

"I would've noticed," Payton agreed with enough offense that Narcisse turned to study xem.

Xe were pale, shaking and so furious that Narcisse wondered just how Chikere and Matija had been killed. Or if their relationship to Payton was a different one than Narcisse had assumed based on their interactions.

"No, not gone-dead," Shani corrected with a tired little wheeze from her spot on the floor of the transport. "Gone-abandoned us."

"Oh, they didn't," Narcisse breathed.

"They did," Payton confirmed. "In the middle of the fight, no less."

Payton's fury seemed absolutely insufficient as pure rage swept through Narcisse. She pulled off the restraints, slipped back into the rear part of the transport and then shoved Payton up into the passenger seat. Xe started but went, leaving Narcisse to hug Shani and mutter curses into Shani's fur.

No one worthwhile could abandon Shani. There was no excuse. None.

Shani's sides shook as she laughed silently at Narcisse's offense on her sake. "Oh, child. They were probably paid off. Or paid too little for the threat."

"I don't care," Narcisse huffed. "I'll never forgive them for this. Traitors."

She shook her head and then turned to Payton who peered back into the transport with a squint that said xe couldn't see either Narcisse or Shani but xe really wanted to. Right. Well. Time to take care of her claws.

"Do you have a knife?" Narcisse asked Payton.

"Really?" Tracey asked, voice all squeaky with horror.

"No time like the present," Narcisse said. "Keep heading east. Maybe we can hide in one of the big resorts. Pretend to be some big important Drath or just take over one of the empty vacation homes for a bit. We will need to find the trackers and I absolutely need to fix my claw problem if we're going to be fighting."

"And we will," Tracey said.

She shuddered and nodded to Payton who frowned before passing a lovely little ten-centimeter holdout knife from xyr boot.

"What are you doing?" Shani asked. Her tail-hand curled around Narcisse's wrist, keeping her from setting her claws against the edge of the blade.

"There's two ways to fix dull claws," Narcisse explained. "One is slow and painless. The other is fast and brutal. We don't have time for the slow method so it's the brutal one. I won't be defenseless, Shani. Not with all these threats to my safety, Tracey's and yours. I think Payton can protect xemself, of course, but I still wouldn't want dull claws if a threat to xem caught up to us."

Tracey steered the transport onwards, hurtling them up the road towards the curve of bay where the big resorts lined the best beach on the island. Those huge buildings with their hundreds and thousands of guests and staff would be a great place to hide.

If Narcisse wasn't halfway convinced that the entire island was in on this attack.

Outside the front window, Narcisse could see tropical palms and flowering shrubs the size of small buildings whipping by. Inside the transport, the only sound was Shani's harsh breathing. Shani's nostrils flared. She nosed Narcisse's cheek, smelling of worry, of fear, of desperate resignation to the fact that she was sick and not healing, trapped and not able to get help.

No. There was help. If not Shani's people, if not Payton's, then Narcisse and Tracey would help. They didn't have much, but they were darn near indestructible and deadly when they wanted to be.

This was not going to happen. One way or the other, Narcisse *would* figure out what was wrong with Shani, and she *would* get Shani back to her people. No other result was acceptable.

Shani huffed and rested her head against Narcisse's for a long moment. Her tail-hand caressed Narcisse's wrist as Shani's scent went so rich and deep with intent that it had to be Shani saying something in her own language.

Narcisse didn't understand it. Not consciously. But she could... feel... the shaky appreciation, the desperate hope, and almost felt like she could get the gist of what Shani said. It was like hearing a quiet conversation through a wall. Bits and pieces were almost intelligible but only the emotion came through clearly.

It was enough.

Shani nodded and let Narcisse go. Her tail-hand curled around Narcisse's back to support her as Narcisse slashed off the blunt claws on her left hand. Blood. Pain, shocking and intense, turned her stomach.

Narcisse wheezed and awkwardly switched the blade into her crippled hand so that she could get her right hand's claws.

Taking all five claws at once sent white-hot explosions through her.

Narcisse collapsed into Shani's side, shuddering and whimpering as she panted her way through the time it would take before her claws healed back up. She couldn't count. Couldn't breathe. Couldn't think or move or do anything but cry as she tried to keep her dinner down.

"What the hell?" Payton demanded over Narcisse's head.

"It hurts to break a claw," Tracey explained. "To lose all of them at once? I'm shocked Narcisse didn't go into convulsions."

"My scent is helping," Shani said as she firmly tucked Narcisse against her side. "Give her a minute. They're healing quickly."

Not fast enough.

They needed to hole up somewhere safe. Somewhere that no one could find them. Preferably somewhere that had good enough medical facilities that they could find any trackers implanted in either Payton or Shani. On their equipment. Whatever.

Narcisse tried to say that, tried to open her eyes, but nothing came out other than a low moan.

Definitely not healing fast enough, damn it. The whistling roar of a flyer on fast approach set Tracey to cursing and Payton to scrambling for xyr weapons. Narcisse shuddered. So not healing fast enough, not when the next round was starting up already.

SIX
FROM SCRAPS AND RAGE

THE PITCH-BLACK FLYER roared up at them. Payton scrambled for xyr blaster, checking the battery and cursing that xe'd already used three quarters of it. Worse, xe didn't have a backup battery. Chikere had been carrying the batteries in xyr pack. Matija had the spare needle packs.

All Payton had was about fifteen needles and a quarter charge.

"We've got to get out of sight," Tracey snapped at Payton.

"They have to be tracking us," Payton agreed. "Where can we hide?"

"Narcisse was thinking about the rich people's mansions up ahead," Shani suggested in a tone that said she didn't think that they'd make it there in time. "Or the resorts."

"Resort it is," Tracey said.

She spun the controls and they crashed into the curb before peeling around a corner that led down a long, broad roadway lined with more of the damned flowering shrubs. Payton hung on, cursing inwardly instead of vocally so that xe didn't disrupt Tracey's concentration.

The resorts in this part of the island were huge buildings the size of a small space station. Each one would easily hold ten or twenty thousand people, guests and staff combined. They'd been painted bright tropical colors, blazing yellow and terracotta red with blue stripes, green stars, all sorts of designs that were the wrong side of garish.

There was no missing the designs. Every single resort had floodlights pointed up at them so that you couldn't avoid looking at them even in the middle of the night.

"Top right pocket," Tracey snapped at Payton. "I've got a chit in there. Pull it, quick."

Payton grabbed for the pocket, blushing at the way Tracey's breast squished under xyr fingers. She had a lot more breast going on than Payton did. A lot more. It made getting the thumbnail sized chit almost impossible but after six seconds too long groping Tracey as she winced and grimly piloted the transport, Payton got it out.

"On the front dash," Tracey ordered.

"Which?" Narcisse asked.

"Eight-Spoke Wheel," Tracey answered, which meant nothing to Payton until she turned sharply into the entrance to the resort that had huge gold-colored wheels painted on the sides of its central tower.

"Oh, good choice," Narcisse said as she slowly pushed herself upright. "Flyer?"

Payton cursed and looked, heart lurching in xyr chest as xe realized that xe'd lost track of the damned thing while groping Tracey.

"Overflew us," Shani reported. "I think it's circling around."

"Good," Tracey said.

The chit flashed once as they reached the barricade blocking the entrance to the resort's parking garage. For a too-long moment, Payton wondered whether or not the chit would work. Then the barricade rolled back, and Tracey drove them into the garage. She parked right next to the main entrance to the resort.

"We're searching for a renegade Drath and their team," Tracey announced. "Narcisse, you're General... what name should you use to get the most attention when people report back?"

"Rrutia," Shani said, ears plastered against her skull and eyes wide. "I can't pretend to be Rrutia!"

"Do it," Tracey snapped at her. "Be all stiff and formal and angry. You know, as angry as you can be. I'll do the talking. Payton, you're my guard. Narcisse, you're translator for Shani. Shani, growls and sneers, no words."

There was no way it was going to work.

Tracey turned to Shani and pointed one imperious finger. "Stiff. Angry. Ears back, ruff up, no looping that tail."

"Got it," Shani said with her ears perked forwards and her tail in loose loops.

Both Narcisse and Tracey glowered at her until Shani sighed and shook herself. She managed not to loop her tail and her ears kept rotating but at least she got her ruff up a bit. This was so going to get them all killed.

"Let's go," Tracey said as she popped the back door of the transport.

Payton went out one side. Tracey went out the other. Both of them startled the porter standing at the door. When Shani jumped out, tail going low and ears satelliting to hear everything in the area, the porter went dead-white.

"General Rrutia requires a suite," Tracey announced so fiercely that she could've been Gensyn getting ready to tear people apart.

"A... what?" the porter asked.

"Is the desk open?" Tracey snarled at him.

Narcisse carefully stepped out of the transport, moving to stand next to Shani. She kept her hands folded loosely and carefully in front of her with the fingers straight so that her fingertips, her claws, didn't brush against anything. The back of her shirt was sweaty. A trickle of sweat trailed down one cheek. Other than that, she didn't show just how much pain she was in.

"Yes, ma'am," the porter said, swallowing hard.

"Good," Tracey snapped at him.

She waved for Payton to take the lead which xe did with xyr weapon at the ready. It meant that Payton got to storm into the lobby, glaring at everyone and everything.

The security system was shit. There were scanners everywhere, of course. All these resorts had them, just as a matter of course. None of them set off alarms at all of Payton's weapons. Even the front desk clerk went still instead of punching the security alert button, a little girl of maybe nineteen with buck teeth and hair pulled back so tightly that it made Payton's head hurt just looking at her.

Payton nodded to Tracey who squared her shoulders and strode straight to the front desk with the sort of stalk that, in other circumstances, would've had Payton propositioning her. She walked like death come calling, like a hunter, like a predator on the prowl and the front desk clerk was dinner.

"General Rrutia requires a suite," Tracey announced. "It must be ground level, have a least three exits out of it, and be soundproofed."

"G-general?" the front desk clerk spluttered. She opened her mouth to protest.

And then snapped her mouth shut with a terrified whine as Shani and Narcisse came in.

"Time is of the essence," Narcisse said in a horribly gentle tone that was a perfect contrast to Tracey's ferocity. "The General apologizes for the disruption but a rogue Drath by the name of Shani has… hm. Well. You're not authorized for that information, sorry. The General requests access to the suite immediately so that the rogue Drath can be captured."

"Oh, shit," the front desk clerk breathed. "Um, um, I need to call my manager."

"Good, do that," Tracey snarled at her. "Every minute counts and you're wasting precious seconds."

The girl slapped her comms and started babbling about generals and angry Drath and getting bitten. The response from her comm was loud enough that Payton had to press xyr lips together to keep from grinning at the sheer chaos claiming to be Rrutia was causing.

They might not be able to get a message back to the mainland to the rest of the Drath, but this should go through the community like a backdraft consuming a section of a space station without good fire suppression. It might, possibly, get them help. At the very least, it should give the others a clue that something was very, very wrong out here.

"Um, my boss, um, says that you can use the executive suite," the girl said. "Right this way."

She ran around the front desk partition and led them off to the right down a dark hallway with stark white walls and echoing tile floors what would do a lovely job of letting Payton know if anyone came this way. Payton took the lead, clearing the suite before letting Tracey, Narcisse or Shani into it. The executive suite was huge, three bedrooms with beds big enough for three Drath of Shani's size to lounge on at a time, an enormous lounging area with a full kitchen that was sterile and empty.

"Good, now get out," Tracey snapped at her.

She waved for Payton to take up a post next to the sliding armored glass doors that led out to the private pool with its own hot tub and an eight-foot-high fence made of tropical wood. Pot lights set into the ground illuminated the private pool area beautifully. Nowhere for an attacker to hide. No signs of hidden weapons, just the standard security setup that would send out alarms if someone jumped into the pool area without permission.

"The General thanks you for your assistance," Narcisse said with a deferential little bow towards the clerk. "She requests that raw meat be brought. Also raw fruit and vegetables, please. About thirty pounds of meat and fifteen pounds of vegetables. Only five or so of the fruit."

"I, uh, yes, ma'am," the girl stuttered before relaying that on through her comms.

By the time Shani stalked, stiff-legged as commanded, into the lounging area, several very frightened waiters came running with rolling trays full of just that. It looked to Payton like they'd grabbed things out of the refrigeration units and thrown them onto beautiful silver platters without an attempt to make them pretty the way these places always did. The fruit was in a basket. The broccoli, squash and sweet potatoes were still in their shipping boxes.

"Thank you very much," Narcisse said with one of her very gentle and deferential bows and a smile so bland that it looked like it had to hurt her face. "The General will inform you if anything else is needed. The General's comms should be sufficient to her needs at this time so we will not require further assistance from your staff."

Tracey promptly shut the door in the girl's face and triggered the privacy protocols.

Blast shields rolled down over the windows. The door locks engaged with a solid thump. The air system hummed and switched to internal filtering which was so much like proper station filtering systems that Payton blew out a breath from sheer relief. All that wild air full of who knew what sorts of pollen always did freak xem out.

"I can't believe that worked," Shani said as she flopped on the floor.

"Neither can I," Payton agreed.

"It won't work for long," Tracey said. "Okay, Narcisse, get over here and eat. Shani, you, too. Both of you need to get your strength up because we're going to be running for our lives soon. Payton, there are trackers on you and Shani. We need to find them, and we need to find them right now."

Payton nodded. "Right. Check Shani's fur and her skin. I'll go through my clothes and equipment. Someone else will have to help me check my back for implants."

"No, we'll start with you," Shani said, shaking her head hard enough to spray loose hair and dander around her. "I'll be… more challenging, what with the fur."

"…Right."

It felt… horrifying… to strip down to xyr skin but Payton didn't see any other way to make sure that xe didn't have trackers in xyr clothes. Xe also needed to let Tracy and Shani check for trackers and skin was better for that.

Still sucked vacuum, hard.

Payton didn't shift all the way, like many Gensyn did on xyr home station. Xe always had tits and a vulva. Xe always had a penis. Payton's shifts were more a matter of emphasis than of transitioning entirely from burly male configuration to hippy female configuration.

Showing xyr genitalia to people that xe had only met tonight, letting Tracey run her fingers over xyr back and arms and legs to check for implants, made Payton squirm.

Tracey didn't even look at Payton's body. There was not one single flicker of interest or curiosity as she searched Payton for the presumed implants. Neither did Shani who just snuffled at Payton and pointed out three trackers that had been implanted just under the skin who knew when. Once pointed out, Tracey grunted and nodded that they were there though she had to poke firmly and then sniff very closely, too, to confirm it.

Narcisse looked at Payton, blank-faced and chewing mechanically with her mango suspended between the palms of her hands so that her fingers wouldn't touch anything.

Given that look, Payton would bet a healthy sum of credits that Narcisse didn't see a damned thing.

Shock-trauma, maybe. Or pain-trauma, more likely. Narcisse's fingertips were swollen and purple, but the color faded as she ate and her distant, unseeing look sharpened the more food she put in her belly.

Her fingernails sharpened, too.

Her claws.

Good. They sure as fuck needed all the weapons they could get.

"Right," Tracey said once she was done marking each implant. "Narcisse, you're better at this. Your claws healed up enough for a little surgery?"

"I think so," Narcisse said, frowning at the pen marks on Payton's hip, thigh and right upper arm. "But my venom will knock you flat for a little while."

Payton shrugged. "I don't mind. It'll give my system a chance to adapt to your venom. Can't help but think that will be a good thing."

And if Payton was really lucky, xe would adapt well enough that xe wouldn't pass out or die if exposed to either of the sisters' venom. Right now, resistance was as useful a weapon as a blaster. After all, who knew what their enemy would throw at them?

Venom might be the least of it.

SEVEN
QUESTIONS IN THE WIND

IT WAS AMAZING what some food could do. Narcisse methodically worked her way through another mango, several slabs of meat that tasted like a cross between beef and tuna, and then about a liter of water that had been stripped of every single mineral by distillation. She grimaced while chugging it down. Why would someone enjoy water that tasted of nothing? So nasty.

Either way, Tracey was as focused as a laser as she carefully checked every single inch of Shani's body. Where Payton had three trackers implanted right under xyr skin, Tracey kept finding them on Shani.

"This one?" Tracey asked for the nineteenth time.

"Mm, no, that's one of ours," Shani said for the eleventh time.

"Your people are both shockingly paranoid and stupidly lax about safety," Tracey complained as she worked her way over Shani's rump. "I mean, not one bodyguard and yet you're covered with trackers of all… this one?"

"Not ours," Shani confirmed, nosing the spot and then nodding with her ears slapped back against her skull. "That one's active, unlike the others so far. We'll have to take it out last."

Narcisse shook her head, went to wash her hands, and then came over to sit next to Payton who'd spent the whole time sitting naked and scowling as xe watched Tracey and Shani. Payton's eyes flicked over to Narcisse who flexed her claws and cocked her head Payton's way. Xe grimaced and then sighed.

"Yes, let's get this done," Payton said.

"No, not yet," Tracey snapped at both of them. "Not until we've located all of Shani's. We're going to have to move fast once we tear them out."

"Clothes," Payton said.

Xe skinned back into xyr clothes so eagerly that Narcisse had to wonder about Gensyn culture. She'd always heard that the Gensyn were casually sensual, open to sex and cuddling and fighting with pretty much anyone. They were, after all, more or less unkillable with their incredibly powerful nanites. There wasn't a disease in the universe that could keep them down and very few weapons outside of mass destruction could stop them.

Payton didn't seem to share that calm, open sexuality. If anything, xe seemed disturbed to allow anyone to see xyr body. Which was odd. Payton was quite appealing physically, lean and strong with defined muscles on xyr arms and legs. Xyr back was like a wall of muscles and xyr trunk was broad and well padded. Narcisse would bet that Payton could hunt for days and fight for hours if xe needed to.

It was amazingly attractive but then Narcisse had always found the hunters, fighters and killers of their world more interesting than the scientists that she spent time around.

Irrelevant, of course, since Payton didn't appear to be interested in sex with anyone, especially not Narcisse. Or Tracey. Narcisse certainly wasn't going to make things any weirder than they already were by hitting on Payton.

By the time Payton had xyr clothes on, weapons checked, stripped of their two trackers, and then strapped back on, Tracey had found a total of thirty-three trackers on Shani. Of those, only twelve needed to be removed right now.

"I do think removing the others might be necessary eventually," Narcisse commented as she flexed her claws and nodded that they were finally back to proper needle sharpness. "There's always the possibility that this is an internal issue. One where your people decided to get rid of you."

"That's… highly unlikely," Shani said, pausing to visibly edit whatever she'd started to blurt before it could escape her mouth. "I will grant that… there may be others tracking those trackers but for now I'd rather keep them. Just to be on the safe side. The paperwork for losing all your trackers is rather overwhelming."

Narcisse grinned, inappropriately amused by the idea of masses of paperwork intimidating the great and powerful Drath. Neither Payton nor Tracey reacted to the comment, so Narcisse made herself drop the grin and focus on what needed to be done.

"I'll need access to your trackers," Narcisse told Payton. "Come sit next to Shani. That way we can move as fast as possible."

"It's all on you, Narcisse," Tracey said. "I've got to be at the security system so I can open everything, and we can bolt as soon as the trackers are out."

She stood and brushed herself off, ignoring the horrified huff Narcisse gave her. Tracey wasn't wrong, but seriously, Narcisse had thought she'd have help getting this done quickly.

"I have a knife," Payton offered. "I can help."

"You'll be out cold," Narcisse said, annoyed at Tracey and the situation and so very worried about Shani who still smelled sore and tired and miserable. "My venom will see to that."

Shani sighed and went to the supply of meat, biting off great, huge chunks of the beef-tuna that she swallowed whole. The pork loins went down in three-pound chunks that Shani didn't chew at all. So did two mangos, one pineapple bitten into half, and a melon that Shani gleefully crunched up and slurped down, leaving wide tooth-tracks through the melon's rind.

"That should help a bit," Shani said as she came back over, flopping next to Payton and Narcisse. She licked her chops and nodded approvingly. "I do like those melons. I'll have to see if we can import the seeds, grow them ourselves. They're nice. Sweet and crunchy."

"Can we focus?" Payton asked.

Xe glared at them all as xe opened xyr uniform so that Narcisse could get at xyr shoulder, side and hip.

"We are focused," Narcisse said. She tugged Payton down and made xem sit firmly in the lounging pit next to Shani. "On making sure that we have the resources to heal as fast as possible."

"I still don't think that your claws will..."

Payton's voice trailed off as soon as Narcisse dug one claw in right under the tracker on Payton's hip. Even though Narcisse did her best not to fill Payton up with venom, it was impossible to hold it all in. The little implant, barely the size of the head of a pin, came out easily. The wound healed up instantly, keeping all of Narcisse's venom inside.

"...aff...eeeect... meeeeee," Payton slurred as xe slumped sideways and passed out cold.

"Hold xem up for me," Narcisse ordered as she tugged Payton's pants back into place.

The other two trackers were the same size and shape. They came out just as easily, too. Narcisse set them aside on one of the bitten-off pineapple leaves. She shivered; a little bit awed that there was no blood whatsoever. Their venom always included an anticoagulant, the better to make their attackers bleed out, but Payton's nanites had beaten it and sealed the wound easily.

"I will not heal that fast," Shani commented as she snuffled at the nonexistent exit wounds. "Though the venom probably won't knock me out."

"Good!" Tracey huffed and her scent went abruptly relieved. "I couldn't figure out how we were going to run if you were out cold."

"You wouldn't," Shani said, sides shaking with silent laughter that looped her tail into a corkscrew. "I'm too heavy for the two of you to carry me, especially if you have to carry Payton and xyr weapons, too."

Narcisse took a deep breath and then found each spot that Tracey had scent marked on Shani's body. Twelve trackers. One active, eleven not active yet. Plus all the other ones that shouldn't, maybe, be a threat to them.

"I am so sorry," Narcisse told Shani. "There's no way to make this painless. And I doubt I'll fast enough to keep you from flinching."

"Do what you need to," Shani ordered.

It was a gentle order, delivered with soft, warm eyes and a loose, resigned slant to Shani's ears, but it was definitely an order. Order or not, the feeling of Shani's hide parting under her claws nearly made Narcisse vomit back up everything she'd just eaten. There was a distinct difference to Shani's flesh, both the tensile strength of hers skin and the roots of her fur binding around Narcisse's claws.

The first tracker came out quickly. Easily. The second was harder. It was as though Shani's body realized that it was being attacked. Her fur stiffened. The down layer went so thick and fluffy that Narcisse could barely get her claws through. When she did break the skin, it aggressively healed around her claws.

"I can't... damn it!" Narcisse snarled as she cut a too-large hole in Shani's hide to get the second tracker out.

"What?" Tracey demanded.

"I can't take them all out, Tracey," Narcisse said. "Shani's body is reacting and defending itself."

"Sorry," Shani said with her ears slapped back against her skull and her tail aggressively still as if she was resisting the instinct to shove Narcisse away. "Just get the active one. We'll work on the others once we're out of here."

"Fuck!" Tracey glowered at Narcisse like it was her fault. "I really wanted them all out."

Getting the active tracker out took eighteen precious seconds, during which Shani panted and shuddered, clinging to the floor with all her clawed toes and with her tail-hand. She growled so ferociously that Narcisse's instincts kicked in. Which, actually, turned out to be a good thing because the shift from sedative to lethal venom let her punch through the stiff fur and into the active tracker.

"It's out!" Narcisse shouted as she dropped the bloody little pea-sized tracker with the others she'd removed. "Get the doors open—I'll get Payton!"

Shani lurched to her feet, favoring her right hind leg which had three bloody patches on it now. Between Narcisse's instincts shouting to run like the wind and Shani's tail-hand levering Payton up off the ground, Narcisse managed to pull Payton over her shoulders in a fireman's carry.

Then they were all out the door and dashing across the perfectly manicured lawn into the darkness beyond the pool's lights. No one was there. No cars waited for them. No flyers. Not even people with weapons set to shot them in the darkness.

In fact, Narcisse didn't smell anyone near them, though she did smell some serious consternation and worry scents from the staff. They'd been sure that Shani was Shani and then Tracey's trick had convinced them that Shani wasn't, and now they were all off somewhere. Presumably trying to determine who Shani actually was.

This head-long bolt into the night was going to prove exactly who they were.

"New vehicle?" Narcisse wheezed as she ran alongside Shani.

"Please," Shani agreed.

"Looking," Tracey called back.

She was in full-on hunt mode, head high and eyes reflecting every hint of light they passed. Narcisse hadn't smelled Tracey this focused in years, not since they were teenage girls hunting in the jungles back home to prove that they were strong and sexy.

It was so much more serious now though.

They ran along the beach, which strangely made Shani terribly skittish, and then crossed a concrete culvert that held a bare two inches or so of water in it. Shani stumbled to a stop at the edge of the footbridge over it. Tracey hissed at her, waving for the two of them to hurry up.

"We need—"

"I know!" Shani snapped at Narcisse.

An actual snap, finger-length claws closing bare fractions of an inch from Narcisse's hand. Narcisse jerked her hand back and then sucked in a breath. This was significant. Very significant. There was something about the ocean, the water, that was a threat.

"Stop being so damned perceptive," Shani complained.

Her haunches bunched and then she leaped straight over the four-meter-wide culvert, disdaining the bridge entirely. Shani's legs collapsed under her when she landed on the other side, but she struggled back to her feet quickly enough that she was up and moving again by the time Narcisse ran across the bridge with Payton flopping over her shoulders.

"Ha!" Tracey's triumph filled the night air.

The truck she'd found wasn't enclosed, not like the last one, but it was big and sturdy and had a canvas top over the back that would shield both Shani and Payton. Better still, it started up silently when Tracey hit the switch. Shani managed to clamber over the high back gate by herself. Narcisse had to lower the gate with one hand to get Payton in.

But once Payton was in the back and the gate was back up, Narcisse ran to the passenger side and climbed in.

"Go!" Narcisse ordered.

"Gone!" Tracey said, grinning with enough defiant victory in her scent that it could've choked Mother at twenty paces.

Possibly because Narcisse was just as triumphant. Even with the wind blowing over the truck's canvas, Shani's quiet relief was a cloud heavy enough to coat Narcisse's tongue. For a long moment, just as long as it took for Tracey to calmly, sedately, drive the big truck out of its shadowed parking place, Narcisse let herself be relieved.

Then she blew out a breath and considered what had happened so far.

The towns were a threat. Whoever was behind this had clearly paid off the townsfolk. That meant that they had to find somewhere to hide out that didn't have lots of people around. Shani clearly, obviously, was afraid of something to do with the water.

Not a little afraid the way she'd been in the restaurant. Not even the faint hints of fear that had come from running through the night. No, the ocean and the water had Shani outright terrified.

The biggest threat was in the water. That meant no boat. They had to find a flyer that they could commandeer and take back to the mainland. If possible.

"Can you pilot a flyer?" Narcisse asked Tracey.

"No~ooo?" Tracey replied, glancing over at Narcisse. "What's with the dire worries about water?"

"Head into the mountains," Narcisse ordered. "We'll have to try to cut across the island's back roads to one of the smaller landing pads, see if we can't steal a flyer."

"Why?" Tracey asked, much more seriously this time.

"I… think that Shani's real enemies are in or on the water," Narcisse explained quietly, well aware that Shani was listening and not replying. Not explaining at all.

Shani's scent went deeply worried, but she didn't say a single word. Tracey and Narcisse exchanged looks.

"Mountains it is," Tracey agreed grimly.

EIGHT
AGAINST AN UNSEEN THREAT

SOMETHING JOSTLED PAYTON'S HEAD. Xe groaned and swiped at whatever it was. Xyr hand impacted a solid, furry surface.

Fur?

What?

Between one heartbeat and the next, everything returned to Payton. Xe sat bolt-upright, flailing for xyr blaster only to wheeze as Shani laid one heavy paw across Payton's chest. Shani pushed Payton right back down on the bed of…

…a truck? A truck going over some seriously bumpy roads by the feel of it. No wonder Payton had been jostled. Whatever this road was, it clearly wasn't paved and there was no maglev built into it. They might be running purely on wheels against the ground which was horrifying. Who knew what that would do to the soil or if they'd get caught in a pothole or mud pit or something?

"How long was I out?" Payton asked Shani whose ears were pointing straight forward, right at the cab of the truck.

Or maybe ahead of it given that it looked like Tracey was driving in silence and Narcisse was a quiet shadow seated next to her. The truck wasn't completely open to the night air. There was a canvas top that came up over both the cab and the back where Shani and Payton lay.

Payton could see glimpses of starlight through the canvas, so it clearly wasn't intended to keep the rain off.

What had Payton futilely pushing against Shani's leg was that xe could hear tree branches or something brushing against the sides of the truck. Every fond that ran over the canvas made the hair stand up on the back of Payton's neck.

"Shani!" Payton snapped when none of them replied.

"Sorry, forgot you couldn't smell it," Shani said, not glancing down at Payton. "About two hours. We're up in the mountains. We're going to try for a flyer to get back to the mainland. I'd like to avoid boats if possible."

That made…

…less than no sense.

"A flyer isn't going to make it to the mainland," Payton said, craning xyr neck to try and see Narcisse properly. Xe got glimpses of the top of Narcisse's head occasionally as the truck bumbled over the rough road.

"Why not?" Tracey asked in a far too tense voice. "Brace yourselves."

Payton clutched Shani's leg as the truck rolled up a sixty-degree angle and plunged down, sideways and skidding, at a forty-degree angle. Xe slipped against the bed of the truck. Shani didn't. She stayed as stable as a boulder set in bedrock, which meant that Payton hung on harder.

"So why?" Tracey asked even though they were still skidding down the too-steep path.

Rock face? Payton couldn't tell, not from the bed of the truck. Xe'd really like being able to sit up, but Shani just shook her head at xem.

"To get to the mainland by flyer, you need one with long-distance engines and fuel tanks," Payton explained. "We checked before we came out here. The flyers on the island are all designed for hopping between islands. To get to the mainland would take three to five stops at different islands to refuel."

"Fuck," Narcisse grumbled with very little heat for how deeply her claws gouged into the seat cushion behind her. "Well, we'll figure it out. I'm fairly certain that Shani can neither confirm nor deny that there are enemies of the Drath on or in the ocean."

Shani's ears went abruptly floppy as her jaw dropped in a laugh. "I can neither confirm nor deny that, yes."

"Which means that there absolutely is some sort of enemy in or on the water," Narcisse continued. "One that actually scares Shani. Not like the attackers that just sort of annoy her. They're irritating little bugs. The water-associated ones get her scent all panicky."

"...Your nose is too good," Shani complained.

"I promise you," Narcisse said, turning back enough that Payton saw her eyes and frowning eyebrows, if nothing else, "that neither Tracey nor I are a threat to you or the Drath, Shani. I can't even explain it. You're wonderful. You're hurting. You need help. I *will not* let you be hurt. It's not in me to allow it."

"And I'm along for the excitement," Tracey agreed with a chortle. "I haven't had a hunt this exciting since that time when we went out without Mom's permission."

"Don't talk about that or we'll end up in a boat with monsters hunting us from sky and water," Narcisse groaned. "Seriously, that was horrible."

The truck abruptly leveled out onto a road that felt almost normal. Smooth enough that when Payton pushed at Shani's leg, Shani let xem go. When Payton sat up, the velvety darkness hid everything from sight. Xe frowned and turned to look out the front window.

Nothing much more. Darkness, a gravel road full of ruts, and more of the endless tropical greenery pushing inwards towards the truck. Payton glowered.

"Where are we?" Payton asked.

"We couldn't remove all the trackers out of Shani," Narcisse said instead of answering.

Except that that was an answer, now wasn't it?

Damn it, why were two random girls from who knew where better bodyguards that Payton's whole troop? They'd been hired specifically to protect Shani and make sure that no one harmed her. There was no reason for Payton to be effectively worthless.

"Stop beating yourself up," Narcisse said far too gently for Payton's pride. "The reason we're more effective right now is that we're wild cards. Unexpected in every way. We don't react the same. We don't think the same. We don't have the same senses or defenses. Whoever is behind this doesn't know what to do with us."

"It won't last," Tracey agreed with a nod that didn't take her eyes off the road for a single second. "I've no doubt that they're trying to figure out where we're from and what we can do. Every time we do something, it's giving them data."

"Which means we need to get the trackers out," Payton said.

"My body reacted to Narcisse's venom," Shani said with a sigh. "She got the active one plus two more."

"Knife?" Payton suggested. "I can dig them out as well as anyone else."

The truck thumped through a series of potholes that felt big enough to swallow Payton whole. Xe barely managed to keep from sliding right across the bed of the truck and out the back gate. It was Shani's muscular tail that saved Payton, whipping around xyr waist and holding xem close to Shani's side.

Because of course Shani didn't move.

"I've got claws, too," Shani said, tail quivering and ears all floppy again. "Not like theirs but enough to punch holes in the bed of this and hang on for dear life."

"...I want claws now," Payton grumbled under xyr breath.

Except not really. Xe never had wanted to do the sort of Alterations that would take. Xe healed, could have or sire whatever babies xe wanted, and xe was strong. That was good enough for Payton.

Though claws really would be lovely on this mission.

No, still not worth it. Not that it mattered at that moment. There was no way Payton could get alterations out in the boonies, even if xe wanted to. Xe grimaced as an especially large spikey frond-thing scrapped against the canvas over the top of the truck. This whole thing was ridiculous, but at least they were all in a truck instead of on foot. Who knew what bugs were out there living in the wildlands surrounding them?

Payton shuddered. Then flinched as the truck went over a hard bump and then up onto smooth paved road. Both Tracey and Narcisse stiffened as if getting ready to leap straight through the windshield at phantom attackers.

"That's an airfield," Payton said, staring at the little grassy landing strip and ragtag support buildings. "With flyers."

There were only a few lights on, but it was enough to illuminate eight short-range flyers with stubby wings and brick-shaped bodies that the locals used for flying tours of the islands. None of the flyers looked to be in great shape. All of them looked to be at least airworthy, if not capable of surviving anything dramatic.

Even better, the airfield buildings were completely dark. Not a single light or vehicle around other than the flyers meant that they had a great chance of getting away with this. Payton shook xyr head, astonished that they'd stumbled on this place.

"We knew it was here," Tracey explained to Payton's unasked question. "We took a flight over the island when we first arrived. It was out of here. That was fun. Lots of cool sights along the way."

"Including several places on other islands where we can take a ship back to the mainland," Narcisse said with a huge grin over her shoulder at Shani, definitely not at Payton, "and several long-range flyer bases that we can try to get at on the next island over."

"...You two are better at my job than I am," Payton complained.

Not that xe was bitter over it, exactly, but xe really was horribly bitter about the entire mess. Xe was supposed to be guarding Shani, keeping her safe, and bringing her back to her people intact. Instead, Payton had lost xyr team, gotten Shani sick and injured, and now had to rely on complete strangers, civilians, to do xyr own job.

It hurt, a bit. But xe hadn't failed entirely yet, so Payton wasn't going to let the bitterness and regret overwhelm xem.

"Nope," Narcisse said with a wry little smile. "We're just better hunters. You're a soldier, a guard. We're predators. Totally different thing."

"Fascinatingly different thing," Shani murmured. "I don't smell anything active. No living people."

Payton turned and frowned at Shani. "Do you smell dead people? Because that's absolutely relevant."

Narcisse had a vaguely horrified expression that twisted to

monstrous fury as the shadows shifted across her face. She nodded and made a garbled noise that most likely was "agreed!" crossed with "very relevant!" Tracey didn't say a thing. She just slowed the truck to a crawl as her fingers went white on the steering wheel. There was a set a tiny popping noises that Payton suspected was Tracey's claws going into the material sheathing the steering wheel.

"Well, yes?" Shani said, ears back. "They're fairly fresh, actually. Probably about… five or six humans, I think? Locals. None of them smell like you, Payton, or either of you, Tracey, Narcisse. The amount of blood makes me think they were bled out."

The dark windows of the multicolored shacks loomed in the night.

Ignition keys would have to be inside there. Xe could, probably, jury-rig one of the flyers to get it started but there was no guarantee that whoever had killed the people Shani smelled hadn't also sabotaged the flyers.

"We can't take the flyers," Payton said.

"They're our best bet," Tracey protested far too weakly to really mean it.

"They're almost certainly sabotaged," Payton said. "I'm good enough to fly one. I'm not good enough to see if one has been sabotaged. I certainly can't fix it."

"Then this is a trap," Narcisse said, glaring at the flyers that were useless to them. "Where's the road go, Tracey?"

"Up around the mountain and then down to the ocean again," Tracey said with her own glare at the shacks.

Payton shook xyr head. "Irrelevant at this point. Trackers have to be first. All three of us have to work to get them out of Shani. Then we can move on from here. Whoever's behind this will expect us to scout the flyers, to clear the shacks. Then move on. If we're careful and quick, we can get the trackers out of Shani, dump them and move on before the people behind this realize it."

"Hope so," Shani murmured so quietly that Payton turned to stare at her.

Her ears were back against her skull, eyes wide and frightened. Payton had never seen Shani this frightened before. Actually, xe had never seen Shani afraid at all, even when she was so sick that she couldn't stand up and every motion made her throw up violently.

So.

Narcisse was right. The people behind this were much more dangerous than Payton thought. Getting Shani back to her people in one piece might be the most important job that Payton ever had.

Xe would have to work extra hard to make sure that all four of them survived it.

NINE
HUNT THE HUNTERS

THREE PEOPLE WORKING to remove trackers at one time made for a mildly crowded surgery, but Shani willingly lay on her belly in front of the truck's lights. It was the best light they had available. It took only about two minutes to get all of the trackers out of Shani, though her fur and hide did fight against Tracey and Narcisse's claws on the last round.

Interestingly, Payton's knife didn't cause the same instinctive reaction, so Payton ended up getting the final two with a quick flick of xyr blade and a deft press of xyr fingers.

Shani shook so hard that a cloud of dander and fur billowed off her, covering all of them. Then she stood up and nodded towards the shacks.

"Are we checking those?" Shani asked.

"No point," Narcisse said. She sighed. "There's no one alive in there."

Narcisse's nose wasn't as good as Shani's, obviously, but the instant they'd stopped the truck and stepped outside, the smell of death and blood was obvious. Blood stink mixed with the smell of lush greenery and ripening fruit on the big mango tree next to the hanger with the safety gear. The stench of death curdled the lovely smell of wet earth.

Wet.

There was a creek behind the shacks. Narcisse had forgotten about that, damn it. She stood and glared at the dark-hidden creek while brushing Shani's fur off. The problem with everything they'd done so far was that they were clearly being herded.

The so-called attempt at the restaurant had been anything but convincing, looking back at it. Shani's nanites and alien biology made it unlikely that a poisoning attempt would be effective. It was an attempt to frighten the Gensyn, which had clearly worked for Matija and Chikere. Payton seemed to be the sort of person who never looked back and never gave up once xe decided to do something.

Either way, the attack in town, the way they were driven to hide and then slip away in the darkness, that was something their opponents had obviously planned. Otherwise Narcisse wouldn't be standing here with the smell of bloody death in her nose.

"They killed those people because we teamed up with you and Shani," Narcisse declared.

"...Probably," Payton said, considering it for a long moment. Xe winced and brushed off, too. "Yes, I think you're right. They knew that you'd been here."

"It wouldn't be hard to figure out," Tracey agreed with one of her truly pissed-off scowls. "We talked about it endlessly over the last couple of days, recommended the flights to a few people."

Narcisse nodded. "So, as soon as we joined up, someone checked on where we'd been and then cut off all our ways off the island. Anything we've been to would have been compromised."

"Probably the whole tour thing we were going to do tomorrow, too," Tracey agreed. "We need to flip the hunt, Narcisse."

"Oh, I completely agree," Narcisse said.

The words came out very softly given how furious Narcisse was about this entire situation. She'd been upset when she met Shani. Now, after all of this, Narcisse was so angry that she could feel her venom sacs in her mouth and fingertips swelling with new venom.

Lethal venom.

The next person she bit or clawed was going to die so very hard. Narcisse breathed slowly, staring at the shadow-hidden creek that would carry their scent on the wind. Anyone with the nose for it would be able to follow them easily. Worse, whoever the enemies were that Shani feared so much, they were water-borne. That meant that wet places were a danger.

And every single place they'd been herded had been wet.

"Inland," Narcisse announced. She turned to Tracey who raised an eyebrow. "We're going dry places, ones where scents don't linger. Somewhere hard, gravel, lava, sand, whatever it takes to disperse our scents instead of gathering them."

"Oh, good idea," Tracey said with a nod. "Shouldn't be too hard. The leeward ridges are nice and dry around here. Steep, but we can work with it, I think."

"Can you keep up at a full run?" Narcisse asked Payton and Shani.

"You can't keep up with my full run," Shani snorted. Her tail was in loose loops at the sheer concept of Narcisse and Tracey outrunning her. "Even this weak, you're nowhere near as fast as I am."

"I will keep up," Payton said so grimly that Narcisse adjusted her plans to account for Payton's weaknesses. "When do we leave?"

No nose to smell threats, no way to see in the dark, no training in hunting over natural, wild ground full of predators; Payton was a definite liability. For now. Once they struck back, began to fight whoever was behind this, Payton would be vital. For now they needed hunters and trackers.

Later they would need Payton to be their soldier.

Their general.

"Now," Narcisse replied because there was no reason to wait and give their enemies to corral them even further. "Shani, stick with Payton. Xe can't see or smell like we can. Tracey and I will take the lead. Tracey's better at scouting. I'm better at hunting. She's first, I'm second. The plan is to flip this hunt on its head. We're finding who's behind it all, on the human side of things, and we're going to wring answers out of them."

"Or kill them," Tracey said cheerfully enough that Shani's tail went into a tight corkscrew and Payton grinned. "Either works."

They left the truck behind with the flyers that had to be tagged and monitored and, probably, sabotaged to be useless for their purposes.

The island's topography was brutal, full of steep gullies that swept up towards the volcano at the heart of the island in near-vertical cliffs. They could've taken the road that ran around the perimeter of the island but that was pointless.

The beaches were where most people lived. That was where all the cameras and monitoring equipment were. Where the people, the humans, were hunting them. That meant going into the wild jungles of the inland and braving those stupidly steep gullies.

"Ridgeline?" Tracey asked about two hours later when they'd made it over the sixteenth ridge and looked out over an older lava flow that had gone cold and dry. "We could head inwards towards the observatory on the minor volcano, whatever its name was."

"Skandar Observatory," Narcisse said, staring over the lava field as they waited for Shani and Payton to catch up to them.

Payton's cursing caried on the wind along with the scent of morning dew forming on the greenery around them. So did Shani's exhaustion and the faintest scent of sea salt which should not have carried all this way up into the mountains. No matter what Shani claimed about being able to outpace them, her health wasn't strong enough for that right now. Which was a problem. A very large problem.

The lava flow was about the same distance away as the observatory. Narcisse bit her lip and then shook her head. There really wasn't a choice.

They should go to the observatory, of course. There would be vehicles there, communication devices. When they toured the observatory after they arrived, the tour guide had talked about the comm systems that communicated with incoming space ships. If they could get access to the comms, that would solve at least half their problems.

"Oh, wait," Narcisse said, turning to Tracey as her stomach sank down to her toes. "We told people about visiting the observatory, didn't we?"

"Well, yeah, but—" Tracey broke off and then cursed a blue streak.

"We are not... going to be able to go much farther," Payton announced with a mildly breathless huff of effort as xe scrambled up onto the ridge with Shani.

Xyr hand was on Shani's shoulder, helping push Shani up the slope to the narrow ridgeline. It was only a meter and a half wide, a knife-edge of stone decorated with low grasses and ferns being slowly worn down by the rain and wind and jungle plants that towered up over them. Thankfully, at the ridge, the spikey palms and shaggy ferns were thin enough to allow Narcisse to see the sun coming up over the ocean to the east.

The sky was red and purple, shading towards gold at the horizon. Very soon, they would be horrifically visible up here on the ridge. Given that Shani's jaw sagged open, her purple-black tongue lolling out as she panted, head and tail hanging low, they needed to go to ground.

Something had to still be on Shani.

Some parasite or poison, some implant that they hadn't caught yet. There was no reason for a Drath with nanites three million years more advanced than anything humanity had come up with to have this much trouble healing. Her sweat smelled like sea salt, exactly like sea salt, until Narcisse got right up close to her. Then Shani's actual sweat-smell overwhelmed the sea salt sweat that couldn't be sweat as it filled Narcisse's nose with bitter almond and hints of cinnamon exhaustion.

Payton was sweaty, but xyr nanites had xem breathing relatively smoothly despite being the slowest and least trained with all this terrain. Xe didn't have the slightest hint of sea salt, just normal human sweat saltiness and acrid frustration.

"We have to go to ground," Narcisse decided. "It's too far to get anywhere useful right now. We need a hiding place, to search Shani's fur again, and scavenge something to eat. That's the priority."

Tracey nodded thoughtfully. "That's a plan. Follow the ridge after me. I'll scout for a good spot to hide. Shani, can you climb trees?"

"...Yes?" Shani said so hesitantly that Narcisse frowned at her. "Yes, actually, I can. Getting down could be a challenge. The ground's a little steep for jumping, but yeah. If I have to."

"Got it," Tracey said.

She ran off up the ridge, head rotating left and right as she scanned and scented for anything that might help them. Narcisse left Tracey to that. She'd always been better at that than Narcisse had.

Shani pressed her head into Narcisse's belly, all but begging for petting. It brought a quiet laugh bubbling up Narcisse's throat as she complied. Shani's fur was wet. Not badly but enough that Narcisse shuddered and pulled her hands away.

"What?" Payton asked as both Narcisse and Shani went still with realization.

"There's too much sweat," Narcisse said as she wiped her hands on a leaf instead of on her pants. "Sorry."

"Someplace enclosed would be nice," Shani said, nodding that they should follow Tracey while her scent filled with fury and outrage that someone could infest her fur with alien spies or tracking devices. "We do like dens."

"There should be caves, maybe lava tubes, around," Narcisse said. "Tracey's good at this. She knows how to scout a location."

Which turned out to be quite true. By the time the sun started edging up over the horizon, sending spears of light stabbing across the island to reveal them on the ridgeline, Tracey came back grinning. She paused, head going up and nostrils flaring as she caught the scent of the sea-salt spies and Shani's fury over it.

Then she grinned and hooked a thumb over her shoulder. "Found a great lava tube that we can hide in. It's nice and big, plenty of head room. It should be a comfy place to spend a few hours while we rest and plan out what to do next."

"Perfect," Narcisse said. "Lead on."

The chosen lava tub smelled like the second or third choice to Narcisse. She caught Tracey's dissatisfaction with the bats that sometimes roosted in the back of the lava tube and the skitter of tiny cave bugs that looked absolutely nothing like cave weta from Old Earth or like the cave millipedes with their stinging tails and biting jaws back home. Harmless little things that seemed far more terrified of them than they were of the bugs, thank goodness.

"I need such a brushing," Shani announced the instant they walked into the echoing opening of the lava tube. "Wow, echoes."

"Yeah," Payton agreed with a scowl. "Seriously, now?"

"Now," Shani insisted while poking her tail-hand at the big knife strapped to Payton's thigh.

Xyr eyes went wide. Narcisse saw the moment where Payton realized that the last layer of trackers was in Shani's fur. Xe winced and turned to Narcisse who held out a hand imperiously.

"As if I'd let anyone else brush Shani," Narcisse said with a proper little huff that made Tracey grin despite the seriousness of the situation. "Goodness, that undercoat of yours has to be absolutely soaked with sweat. Let's see if I can tease a bit of it loose so you don't die of pure heatstroke."

Tracey took a second knife. So did Payton whose hands did not shake in the slightest, despite licking xyr lips nervously.

This had to be done quickly. Very quickly. Narcisse didn't know how close they would have to cut, but she suspected that they would nick Shani several times. Maybe many times. Either way, whatever was hurting her was in her fur, so the fur had to go.

TEN
LIKE DEATH FROM THE SHADOWS

OF ALL THE weird things that Payton had had to do since taking this job for Shani, shaving a Drath down to her skin had to take first prize. Seriously, the Drath were proud as fuck of their fur. Payton had seen them sneer at each other, back before they came out to this damned island, because one of the Drath had rumpled fur or another had brushed too much and looked too sleek, somehow.

Shaved had to be an absolute horror for Shani.

"Now," Narcisse said.

She and Tracey surged at Shani, dragging their borrowed blades close to Shani's skin. They stripped of whole stripes of fur but left great patches behind. Payton shook xyr head and shoved them both away.

"That's not how you get the undercoat out," Payton scoffed at them. "Shani, work with me here. Should only take about a minute and a half if I work quick."

"...Time that," Shani said, ears going cockwise and tail looping in obvious amusement at Payton's confidence.

"All right, go," Narcisse said, eyes on her watch.

Sheering a Drath wasn't appreciably different than sheering a sheep. A lot bigger, yes, and Shani's fur was way less kinky than the sheep Payton's home space station had bred when xe was a child. Didn't matter, though, because Payton knew sheering.

Xe skimmed the knife along Shani's skin, following the contours of her body and manipulating her so that the fur rolled down Shani's body like stripping a bodysuit off. Thankfully, while Shani's outer coat was strait and long, the undercoat was nicely fluffy. The individual strands locked together beautifully which let Payton peel Shani's fur right off her hide.

The bit around Shani's ankles took more care. So did the bit on her belly around her genitalia which Payton never, ever wanted to be that close to again. But it took about a minute and a half and a quick swipe of Payton's knife around the base of Shani's tail to get the last of the fur off of her. Shani's tail, thank everything deemed holy in the universe, only had the finest of fur that was maybe three millimeters long. No need to shave that off.

The instant Shani stepped away from her pile of fur, bunched muscles and lean flanks revealed, Narcisse grabbed Payton and flung xem towards the entrance of the lava tube. Tracey raced past them, and Shani leaped into a run that took her out of the lava tube and down the sloping ground so fast that it was like she'd teleported away.

"What--?" Payton started to ask only to gasp and run for xyr life as the bundle of Shani's sheared-off fur abruptly twisted and flung out long white tendrils that smacked into every living thing in the area.

Trees, ferns, those creepy little bugs with their tripod legs and bulging eyes. Payton flung xemself down the steep slope, uncaring if xe tumbled and fell because no fucking way was xe going to be stabbed by the whatever it was that had been hiding in Shani's fur.

Which Payton was covered in.

Xe cursed and slapped the fur off xyr uniform, shaking as xe skidded down a loose scree of pumice and then smacked into a tree. Narcisse was right next to Payton. She helped remove the last of the fur covering Payton's arms.

Then they ran hellbent through the forest.

Payton could barely keep up with Narcisse. It took xem way too long, several desperate seconds, to realize that Narcisse was going slow specifically so that Payton wouldn't fall behind. Tracey was long gone. There was no sign of Shani at all, not even a bent fern or a print in the fine pumice that they raced over.

"Where?" Payton gasped to Narcisse.

"Further," Narcisse answered, barely breathing hard at all, which was exactly as shame-inducing as it should be.

Xe always liked to think that xe was one of the fittest, strongest people around. Payton trained harder than most Gensyn who, in general, trained harder than any other race of humanity. They were all fighters, all soldiers, all deadly.

Added to that, Gensyn were virtually indestructible. There was no real way to kill Payton. Stab xem, shoot xem, try to bleed xem out, it wouldn't work. Even if someone managed to remove a full limb or drain most of Payton's blood, xyr body would shut down into a stasis sort of condition rather than dying. Hell, if xe lost too much blood adding fluids would bring xem right back.

Payton was strong and deadly.

Supposedly.

All three of Payton's companions in this hellscape of a vacation island were stronger, more dangerous, and had more stamina. It was painfully humiliating.

Narcisse grinned. "Heavy grav world. You're doing good for someone not from a heavy world, Payton."

Payton huffed and glared at her. "Not... helping!"

Even though it did. Payton's home station was slightly heavier than Old Earth standard, but not by an appreciable amount. After this was all over and Shani was safe, because Payton wouldn't accept any other result, Payton was going to go spend a few months to a year or two on a heavy grav station specifically to bulk up and be able to run like Narcisse did. Maybe take special training to hunt like this, too.

Narcisse was outright terrifying as she moved through the tropical.

She leaped over fallen trees as if they weren't there. The occasional gully they went over instead of around was no boundary to her. Narcisse just leaped and landed as if the forty- and fifty-degree slopes were nothing to be concerned about. When the sky began to lighten, Narcisse switched her path so that they were running between the spikey trees and shrubs instead of up on the ridge.

Which meant that Payton kept sliding down the steep incline, cursing under xyr breath, but if that was what they needed to do then that was what they needed to do. Hopefully. Payton really hoped that it wasn't just Narcisse enjoying an early morning run.

"Here!" Narcisse called as she grabbed Payton and flung xem towards a particularly thorny patch of shrubbery.

It wasn't until Tracey's hands and Shani's tail snaked out to grab Payton just before xe got a face full of thorns that xe realized that it was their new hideout.

Only after Payton scrambled into the much, much smaller lava tube with Narcisse on xyr heels did the sound of flyers come clear in Payton's ears. Xe cursed and scrambled up the lava tube with Tracey clinging to one arm and Narcisse to the other. Shani darted ahead, perfectly comfortable in the rapidly absolute darkness. Both Narcisse and Tracey were sure-footed at Payton's sides, damn it all.

"I hate… being helpless…" Payton panted.

"Little further," Shani called back. "Just up here. We should be deep enough that the stone will block any heat or life sign scanners."

Which, yes, Payton should have considered. Along with a thousand other things that xe should have thought of long before this point. Trackers in Shani's body and in her fur, the way that their opponents were so far ahead of them on every single point, xyr teammates bailing and running away instead of staying by xyr side for the fight; every single thing that had happened was something that Payton should have thought of and been prepared for.

Training. So much training. Payton wasn't going to be caught flat-footed again.

"All right," Shani murmured once they stumbled to a stop so far up the lava tube that no light whatsoever came from the entrance. "I think we're in the clear. I can't smell anything anyway."

"No water in here," Narcisse said. "That's good.

"Why?" Tracey asked before Payton could do more than carefully ease into a crouch to pat round xyr feet to see what the ground was like. "I wouldn't sit, Payton. There's lots of those little bugs."

"Ugh!" Payton complained, standing right back up and brushing xyr fingers off on xyr pants.

"I can't tell you," Shani said as if she hadn't been interrupted.

"I can guess," Narcisse said. "Or build a theory based on the knowledge I have at hand, anyway."

"Do," Payton ordered. "I need to understand what's going on and we appear to have some time."

The thrum of the flyer's engines doubled, then quadrupled as multiple flyers went over the area. Payton really hoped that they didn't have advanced scanners. The really powerful ones used by spaceships to scan virgin worlds would pick them up easily. Lucky for them, those scanners were too big to put on a flyer, especially the little ones used on the islands.

"Okay," Narcisse said in a low murmur that was just barely audible over the thrum of the flyer engines, "the Drath are the oldest spacefaring alien species. This is a fact. They're not the only ones. Humanity is the youngest and we used stupid technology to get to the stars."

Shani snort-laughed. "That's one way to put it. Seriously, no one uses generation ships. It's ridiculous."

"My point," Narcisse said entirely too cheerfully. "There are other intelligent species. I think there's five or six of them."

"...Six," Shani replied more slowly.

Slowly enough to make the hair stand up on Payton's arms.

"One of them is water-dwelling," Narcisse said. Paused for a reply from Shani and then hummed when she got nothing whatsoever. "I suspect that they're colony-builders, too. Of course, they would choose worlds that have large oceans, and they probably do their version of terraforming on them, like we do."

"Like this world," Payton whispered, heart lurching in xyr chest at the idea of having to fight super-intelligent fish. Or whatever they were.

"Like this one," Narcisse agreed. "One of the tours we did was a glass-bottom boat that let us glimpse some of the radically diverse sea life in the ocean."

"It was amazing," Tracey commented. "The tour guide said that there's something like eighty percent more sea life than should be there given the life on land and the developmental stage of this world."

"That means... this is a terraformed world," Payton said.

Shani whined. "We're not supposed to tell humans about this!"

"Well, I suspect that they're not supposed to attempt to kill you, either," Narcisse snapped.

Payton would've bet solid credits that Narcisse was glaring furiously at Shani but the darkness in the lava tube was too complete for xem to see anything at all. Xe'd heard that being in the dark was supposed to make your hearing and other senses better. Despite the total darkness, Payton didn't feel like xe could hear better or smell anything other than the dusty smell of the lava tube mixed with xyr own sweat.

Shani sighed. "No, that's not supposed to happen."

"Right," Payton said. "So we've got alien fish—"

"Squid," Shani interrupted.

"Squid hunting Shani," Payton said. "They're somehow controlling or corrupting the humans on-planet and blocking any communications to the mainland. We don't have transportation. We don't have sufficient weapons. We don't have a resupply of ammo."

"That about covers it, yes," Shani agreed with a gusty little sigh. "And I've been shaved."

"Sheered," Payton corrected. "You still have some fur. It's just very short."

All three of them laughed at the distinction but it was a significant one. While Shani didn't have long fur, she had enough left to protect her against the sun and to blunt the thorns and sharp-edged leaves of the plants on the island.

"It's a good point," Narcisse said. Her hand patted Payton's shoulder which nearly made xem leap right out of xyr skin. "Sorry. I keep forgetting that you're totally blind."

"...You can see?" Payton asked with a sense of betrayal as deep and as wide as the entire solar system.

"Mmm, more or less," Narcisse said. It sounded like she shrugged, just from the tone of her voice. "We can see heat patterns, anyway. The bugs in here are cold enough that they're just little shadows but everyone else shows up clearly."

"Footprints, too," Tracey agreed. "We can see Shani's prints all up the tube. How long are we sticking around here?"

"Until I can't smell or hear those flyers anymore," Shani replied so firmly that Payton snapped to attention automatically. "We'll probably have to wait until dark to head out again. Do we know where we're going?"

"Back towards the shore," Narcisse said just as authoritatively as Shani. "The observatory is a bust. Tracey and I went there and told people about how amazing it was. We need to find a place we haven't been and that means going to the north shore nearest to the volcano flows. That's the one thing we hadn't done."

"We were very, very clear about not going there," Tracey agreed. "Too much sulfur. It'd mess with our noses, so it wasn't worth it."

Payton shut xyr eyes and breathed slowly, carefully suppressing the desire to reject that option outright. Right now, Narcisse, Tracey and Shani were what was keeping the four of them alive. Their senses were the key to all of their survival. Going somewhere that would knock all three of their noses out of commission was blindingly stupid.

It might also be the only way for them to get the hell off of this island.

"Right," Payton said. "We should try to rest, somehow. Let's see if we can get the bugs to leave us along long enough to sleep in shifts. The more rested we are, the better chances we'll have."

Not that they had much of a chance at all as it stood.

ELEVEN
QUIET IN THE DARKNESS

RIGHT AROUND NOON as tendrils of warm air slowly wafted up the lava tube like a red, glowing mist on the ceiling and cool blue air crept outwards along the floor, Narcisse sighed and shifted against Payton's shoulder. She really wished she could sit down already.

There was no way she was sitting down.

The stupid bugs were so very annoying because nothing they did would keep the little critters away for long. Chasing them, stomping feet, throwing rocks, stomping on them and crushing their crunchy little tripod bodies, none of it worked. The bugs just came bouncing back after a little while. At least they didn't climb the walls. Or on Narcisse.

While Shani had decided that she'd just deal with them crawling all over her, Tracey had tried sleeping standing up for a while. After an hour or so, she'd given up and flopped on top of Shani and buried her face in Shani's shorn fur so that the bugs wouldn't get on her face.

Tracey was asleep about five minutes after that, darn her anyway.

Even Shani's restless tail endlessly brushing off the bugs away didn't make Tracey stir. She always slept so soundly. Totally unfair of her. That left Payton and Narcisse to stand watch. Literally. They'd planted themselves back-to-back so that they braced each other and then settled in to wait until Tracey and Shani had enough sleep.

"I am so not looking forward to lying down," Narcisse whispered.

"I'd rather sleep standing," Payton replied.

Xyr voice went low, rumbling through Narcisse's back. That last few hours, Payton had been very high-pitched indeed, which Narcisse couldn't blame xem for. Running for your life from pitched battles and wild manhunts had a way of terrifying anyone, but Narcisse had almost forgotten that Payton's voice could go that deep.

"Why are you so determined to protect Shani?" Narcisse asked after a long moment of relative silence, other than the clicking of the bugs and the swish of Shani's tail slowly clearing them from her and Tracey's flanks.

"It's my job," Payton said as though that was an answer.

"No, really," Narcisse said. "Matija and Chikere both cut and ran without shame. I don't see why you didn't, too? I mean, I know why I'm here. I know why Tracey is. I just don't understand why you stayed."

Payton snorted. "Why are you here? There's no reason for you to be so dedicated to Shani."

"I fell in love at first sight," Narcisse admitted without shame. "I'd never let Shani go off by herself. She's fierce and deadly and so smart and kind and gentle and it's... she's perfect! How could I walk away?"

Payton rolled xyr shoulders enough to glance back at her. Narcisse's cheeks went hot enough that even Payton's night-blind eyes should be able to see her blush. Not that Payton smelled like xe could see anything but that hardly mattered when Narcisse blushed this hard.

"I hope that's not sexual interest," Payton said.

"Ew," Narcisse complained just a bit too loudly. "Don't be gross. Sex is sex. Shani is something else entirely. My people don't really think of relationships the same way. You love who you love. You mate with whoever makes sense on the genetic level. Procreation is different. Heck, making babies and having sex are two different things."

Both Shani and Tracey grumbled and shifted around a little. Narcisse huffed, shutting her mouth firmly so that she wouldn't go off on a huge, long lecture about the differences between modes of attraction and how high-danger evolutionary branches of humanity tended to have very different thought process about what constituted a relationship.

"Huh," Payton murmured a good five minutes after Shani and Tracey settled back down to sleep. "I didn't realize that other planets did the same thing we did."

"Gensyn do that, too?"

"Oh, sure," Payton agreed entirely casually. "Sex is... mostly just good athletic fun. Procreation is carefully controlled and very seriously planned. Child rearing is a group activity, usually for extended family structures or for a whole station working together. Love? That's personal and rarely has anything to do with procreative planning. I just... hadn't heard of anyone imprinting on the Drath that way."

Narcisse snort-laughed at that. "I'm sure it's happened. No one's talked about it yet, but it has to have happened. Humans make friends with personable rocks and random bits of fabric, much less highly pettable aliens with amazing senses of humor."

"If you say so," Payton said, shoulders shaking with silent laughter.

Xyr scent went fiercely amused at Narcisse and her crush on Shani. At least Tracey got it. Mostly. Tracey was just as amused by Narcisse's crush on Shani as Payton was, but for Tracey her amusement smelled of "this again?" and "my big sister is so predictable" instead of "high pettable is a non sequitur" and "you have a weird sense of humor".

Narcisse sighed and let it go. It didn't really matter if Payton and Tracey got why Narcisse had fallen head over heels in love with Shani. She had. Shani was fondly stunned by it as well as shyly pleased. The only opinion that mattered was Shani's.

She was, sadly, rather wary about the whole thing, but the complex knot of scents around her thoughts on Narcisse's crush were thick with the taste of governmental requirements and stupid bureaucrats. Shani didn't object because of Narcisse or her own feelings; it was purely because someone among the Drath politicians above her would object.

Too bad. Narcisse was still unreasonably fond of Shani. She was still going to get Shani to safety one way or another. The Drath politicians could go pound sand.

"Do you think we could get to a boat?" Narcisse murmured about an hour later.

"Probably," Payton said thoughtfully. Xyr scent went thick with plotting about how and where, sizes and something that tasted of width and depth that Narcisse didn't recognize. "We'd have to make sure that it was a big enough boat for the four of us. Shani is heavier than she looks."

"So are Tracey and I," Narcisse said, frowning up the tube towards the distant entrance. The bugs were clicking and bouncing deeper into the darkness, away from the heated air slowly drifting down from the ceiling of the lava tube. Good. Maybe they would go away and let Narcisse sleep without bugs crawling all over her.

"Huh," Payton grunted. "Then we'll need something fairly substantial."

"One of the lava flow viewing ships?" Narcisse suggested. "We were really firm about not going there because it would mess with our noses."

Payton turned xyr head, xyr scent of total blindness not lifting at all. "Huh."

"Shani, too?" Narcisse asked.

"Yes." Payton hummed. "The boats that go out to view the lava flows are very popular. It'd be hard to get at them. Also, the marinas in that part of the island are... busy. Lots of people coming and going. We're all going to be on a dozen or more watch lists. No, what I was thinking was that when we were planning this mission, Chikere mentioned that a lot of the houses of rich people are right on the water. They have their own boat docks and their own boats. Many of them are big enough to make the trip to the mainland."

"Now that's promising," Narcisse said, delighted. Then frustrated. "If we can get them."

"That'll be the challenge, yes," Payton agreed. "It's one I think we might be able to meet, though."

"Hope so," Narcisse whispered.

She looked over at Shani. The darkness of the lava tube just made Shani's heat signature stand out that much more brightly. Where the bugs were little dim lavender blobs moving firmly away from the incoming heat and Tracey was a lavender-red lump wrapped with lavender-blue clothes, Shani was golden-red.

Hot. Fever hot mixed with a much higher body temperature made Shani into a shimmering sun sprawled out on the lava tube floor. The bugs didn't avoid her, though. They bounced right at Shani and only moved aside if her tail got too close to brushing them off.

Which was odd if the bugs responded strictly to the heat.

Narcisse stiffened, making Payton tense as well. "Do you have sensor packs?"

"No," Payton said. "Chikere had those. We didn't see a reason to carry redundant gear on a tourist trip."

"That was dumb," Narcisse said instead of cursing the way she wanted. "Stay put. I'm waking Shani and Tracey."

"Why?" Payton asked. Xe clutched Narcisse's elbow blindly, scent ferociously worried without any sign that xe'd known where to grab Narcisse.

"The bugs are fleeing the heat coming up the lava tube," Narcisse explained as she watched the heat slowly drifting towards them. "They're not avoiding Shani and she's hotter than the incoming air."

"Toxins?" Payton asked, proving that xe was just as paranoid as Narcisse was.

"Maybe," Narcisse confirmed.

Payton let go, standing there in what was to xem complete darkness and near silence without a single complaint. Xyr scent went determined instead of frightened or worried. Narcisse nodded at Payton, even though xe couldn't see it, because this was exactly what they needed to get Shani to safety: complete commitment to the job and zero hesitation to act.

Tracey groaned when Narcisse shook her awake. "It can't be time."

"Almost is," Narcisse said, "but that's not why I woke you. The bugs are acting weird."

Shani woke with more difficulty. It took a bit of petting and shaking before she stirred, licking her chops and yawning so widely that her teeth gleamed white-gold and hot in the darkness. Narcisse frowned and cupped Shani's cheek.

"Are you feverish?" Narcisse asked, brushing off some of the bugs that'd clambered up onto her feet as she knelt next to Shani.

"A little," Shani said. "Why? You're a bit early."

"Do you smell anything coming in?" Narcisse asked, which made both Tracey and Shani freeze. "The bugs are acting weird. They don't avoid your extra-high body heat but they're heading up the lava tube as if the heat drifting in from outside is a problem."

Shani rolled to her feet, shaking hard enough to send up a cloud of fur and dander that hung in the air around her like a cloud for a long moment. That cloud was eerily similar to the head coming in from outside. There was a similar sort of weight to it, though the cloud clustered near the ceiling and Shani's cloud of fur slowly drifted to the floor.

"Kneel," Shani ordered. "There is something there."

Tracey was down to her hands and knees instantly. Payton took a moment longer. Narcisse, of course, hadn't yet stood up.

"Is this a human-style threat or a undersea alien can't-tell-you-about-it threat?" Narcisse asked.

Shani snort-laughed as her ears went back and back and back until they were plastered against her skull. At the same time, her tail tucked under her body and then curled around her waist like she wanted a hug and was too afraid to ask for one.

No answer.

Not that Narcisse needed one. As Payton started cursing under xyr breath, xe obviously didn't need an answer either. Tracey scooted over to tug at Narcisse's sleeve. She nodded up the lava tube, away from the opening with it's lighter than air toxic threat.

The bugs were mostly gone now, only a few bouncing along as they escaped from whatever it was that threatened them all.

"We need to go deeper," Narcisse said.

"Further?" Payton complained even though xyr scent was a muddle of resigned and unsurprised.

"There's probably a way out in a connecting tube," Shani commented as she sidled backwards, eyes still locked on the slowly approaching heat signature. "I mean, there almost has to be."

"Seriously, even if there isn't, we need to keep away from this until nightfall," Narcisse said. "Tracey, help Payton. I'll scout ahead this time. I have more cave experience than you do."

"By one day!" Tracey protested. She huffed and caught Payton's sleeve, then xyr hand. "I only missed one day of that expedition."

Narcisse grinned at her, brushing a hand over Shani's shoulder as she stood in a crouch that should keep her head well below the level of the toxic alien cloud of whatever it was. "Still counts. Hopefully we'll be able to stay clear until nightfall or dawn. If we hang out long enough, we should be able to give them the slip."

She wasn't sure she believed that, but it was their best bet for the moment: keep moving, keep hiding, find a way off the island and then get back to the mainland. There were worse plans. For now, this would just have to be enough.

TWELVE
RED SKY AT DAWN

A FULL DAY and half the night hiding in lava tubes full of creepy bugs was enough to give Payton a deep appreciation for the spikey plants that covered this hellscape of a planet. Xe would've preferred to emerge to sunlight, reinforcements with heavy weapons, and a space-worthy launch vehicle, but xe'd take fresh air, open skies fading from purple into indigo darkness studded by diamond stars, and none of the damned bugs trying to climb all over xyr feet.

"See anything?" Narcisse asked in a low voice that barely carried the half meter from her to Payton.

Xe shook xyr head. "Nothing. Smell anything?"

"Moisture on the wind, salt spray, and the jungle, but that's it," Narcisse said far too grimly for it to be an all clear.

"We have to go to the ocean," Payton said, frowning at her. "It's the only way off the island. There's no chance we'll get a flyer capable of long-distance flight on this island."

"I know, I know." Narcisse sighed and rubbed her face with both hands. "I just don't like it. We know the enemy is in the ocean."

"And that we can't do a damned thing about them or their tech," Tracey said from the entrance to the lava tube. "So quit fussing. We should get running. If we're going to make it to the coast, we need to move fast and hard."

Narcisse nodded, but she moved to hug Shani first. The hug made Shani's ears go floppy and her tail curl in loose loops before she patted Narcisse's back fondly. Payton checked all of xyr weapons, what few xe had, and then nodded to Tracey to take the lead as she had before.

There one moment, gone in a quiet shift of the spikey plants around them, Tracey went. Payton followed her with Narcisse at xyr side. Shani started out loping casually by their sides, then she stretched her legs and disappeared into the night like a ghost.

If Payton had any pride left, it would've been decimated by the run through the night.

The stars and moons overhead did nothing to light Payton's footsteps. Xe couldn't see a damned thing. After the second time xe nearly tripped on a hidden rock or branch or whatever it was, Narcisse huffed and pulled Payton to a stop.

"You're slowing us down," Narcisse said. "Dangerously."

"Well, unless you can carry me down the hillside on your shoulders, I don't see what we can do about that," Payton complained.

Narcisse hummed thoughtfully enough that Payton groaned.

Being carried through the dark across someone's shoulder, ass in the air and arms wrapped around xyr head was a thousand times worse than running and tripping and falling down cliffs. A million times. What made it even worse was that Narcisse barely breathed hard. She just hefted Payton and dashed off as if Payton weighed next to nothing.

Heavy grav mods. Xe was absolutely going to get heavy grav mods once xe got home. This was ridiculous.

And effective.

Narcisse and Payton flew down the hillsides so fast that it seemed like Narcisse's feet barely touched the ground every twenty or thirty meters. Every so often, Payton got a fleeting glimpse of Shani running with her tongue lolled out and her ears back, joy radiating in the looseness of her lips and intent in the stiff sway of her tail that acted like a stabilizing gyroscopic rudder during every leap.

Tracey was nowhere to be seen. Not that it mattered, because

Narcisse and Shani followed her invisible trail, her scent trail, as easily as if they were running on a dead-level track with not one bit of vegetation higher than a centimeter off the ground.

Twenty-seven minutes after Narcisse picked Payton up, she slowed and then set Payton back on xyr feet with a grin and a sympathetic pat on Payton's shoulder. Payton wheezed, straightened up and looked around.

Tracey lurked in the shadows a half-dozen meters away, sniffing the air next to a chain-link fence with a gleaming illuminated thread running through it that promised a heavy stun at the least and deadly electrocution at worst to anyone who touched. The darkness was deep enough that Payton couldn't make out what was beyond the fence other than some low, heavily pruned shrubs decorated with glowingly white flowers. Not much of a scent to them.

Actually, there were a couple of things xe could smell as xe stood there: the stench of low tide killing small sea creatures and the sulfur of lava somewhere off to the right.

Shani stalked out of the darkness, moving a good bit better than she had been. "There's no one around. I checked."

"Empty house or research center or what?"

"House," Tracey confirmed. "It's got some serious sensors and stuff on the grounds. The fence is nasty, probably lethal shock levels. But I can smell a boat out there, a nice big one."

"There are other houses around here," Narcisse commented while staring off to the right, "but I don't think it'd be a good idea to go to them. The lava flow is less than half a mile from here. The only reason we aren't choking on fumes is that the wind is blowing them away."

Payton shook xyr head. "That's in our favor. It's probably why the house is empty right now. Okay, I can do something about the fence, but you'll need to be quick. My method won't keep it down for long. Is there an opening or are we going to have to go over the fence?"

All three of them frowned at Payton who just shrugged. As it turned out, there was a small gate through the fence. It was, predictably, securely locked with an electrified deadbolt that would lock the thing shut if the current was interrupted. Payton smiled and nodded.

"Perfect," Payton said. "I'll handle the current. You get the gate open and go through, then pull me through once Shani's in."

"How are you going to handle it?" Narcisse asked with obvious fascination. "These systems are so hard to break. I didn't think you had the tools for that on you."

Payton snorted. "Tools? I don't need tools. I'm Gensyn."

Xe strode over, grabbed the thread on one side of the door in one hand and then grabbed the thread on the other side in xyr other hand. Electricity arced straight through Payton's body, making xem grunt and grit xyr teeth. Fortunately for Payton and unfortunately for the owner of this place, the thread was placed head-high on the fence. Made it much easier for Payton to lean back and away so that the girls could get the door open.

Behind xem, Shani gasped and then barked something in Drath that had to be profanity for how angry it sounded. Tracey's cursing went through eight different languages in her horror and fury. Narcisse?

"I suppose I see why you didn't warn us," Narcisse sighed. "Right. One open door coming up."

Narcisse carefully edged around Payton without touching xem and then kicked the center of the door hard enough that the lock squealed as the hinges broke. The door flew into the yard and clattered to the ground. Then she grabbed Payton's uniform as Payton let go of the now-broken thread.

"I meant... for you... to pick... the lock," Payton complained. "Damn it all. Now... they'll know we're... here."

"Well, you went for the brute force method," Narcisse complained right back at xem as she half-carried Payton with an arm slung around xyr waist and the other over Narcisse's shoulder through the fence towards the house hidden in the darkness, "so I assumed that was what we were going for."

The house, once they got to it, was one of the big, beautiful houses that stupidly rich ground-pounders built to make themselves feel better about their life choices. It was up on thick concrete pilings with hammocks draped between the pilings and mock-rustic couches that looked like they were woven out of native twigs.

A huge outdoor kitchen sat off to the left side of the ground level and several big chests waited on the right. Probably full of expensive diving gear and water sport toys that no one in their right mind would spend money on. Payton let Narcisse drop xem into one of the couches and then snort-laughed as Narcisse glowered down at xem.

"I'm fine," Payton said. Xe wiggled xyr fingers at her. "See? I'm Gensyn. It takes much more than that to kill me. You're stronger and faster than me, not less killable."

Narcisse huffed. "Fine, I suppose you're right. It's just... horrifying. That whole casual electrocution thing you did."

Payton shrugged and let her grumble about it. If xe'd realized that Narcisse would go that route instead of properly opening the door, xe would've just kicked it open xemself. Didn't matter, not really. They would inevitably have people coming after them soon so they would just have to get a move on.

"I've got a lock breaker," Payton said to Tracey as she stalked by. "Wouldn't work on that gate but it should work to start the boat no matter what keys or codes it requires."

Xe pulled it out of xyr pocket and passed it over, smiling as Tracey nodded and then ran off to the dock where the big old boat waited. At least Payton thought it was an old boat. The paint wasn't peeling and the portion of the hull above the water didn't look like it was prone to leaks, but the boat didn't have the shiny newness that xe'd associated with the boats they'd taken to get here.

"There's food," Shani said as she rummaged through the outdoor kitchen. "Water, sealed packages of... something. I think it's supposed to be meat, but I wouldn't place bets on it."

Narcisse joined her and hummed. "Ham. Some cooked bacon, too. Oh, and some roast beef. Looks like sandwiches. They must have been planning on coming back soon. Let me see what I can gather up and we'll all eat."

Shani delivered water in clinking glass bottles. Then Narcisse came back with a mound of meat for Shani and several sandwiches for Payton. She trotted off to deliver some to Tracey, holding them for Tracey to eat as she worked on getting the boat going.

"I am," Shani paused, ears back as she eyed the brightening horizon or perhaps the sea itself, "not very happy with this plan."

"We have to get off this island," Payton replied around a bite of sharp cheese and rich ham slathered with delicious mustard with a smokey tang to it. "We'll die if we stay, Shani. Especially you. We must get out of here. There's no chance otherwise."

"Communications equipment?" Shani suggested even though her tail and ears drooped hopelessly.

"I'll look," Payton said before cramming the rest of xyr sandwich into xyr mouth.

The house up on the stilts was a comfortably comfy version of a rich person's hideaway. There was a comm system, but it didn't connect to anything off the island without a specific key. Payton grumbled and headed down to the dock to retrieve xyr unlocker. The boat, thankfully, was running. Fitfully and obviously not with enough power to get them the hell out of here quickly, but it was running.

"Comms?" Payton asked.

"Short range only," Narcisse complained. "In the house?"

"Locked."

Tracey promptly passed the unlocker over, so Payton left the sisters to work on getting the boat running as well as possible. The comm system, once unlocked, could connect to space but not reliably to the mainland.

"That's not natural," Shani murmured.

"No, it's certainly not," Payton agreed as xe sent a fast SOS straight up into space. Xe put the highest urgency on it and then set the comm system to keep screaming about Drath in danger.

"Let's go," Shani said.

Her head came up as her tail tucked under her belly again. Payton didn't need to hear the flyers to know that their hideout had been discovered. Tracey and Narcisse's cursing from the dock was more than enough to make it clear.

Xe ran down the stairs four at a time, weapons out and Shani on xyr heels.

Time to go.

THIRTEEN
STORM BREAKING OVERHEAD

"OKAY, POWER," Narcisse said as she settled the last cleaned and properly gapped relay back in place.

The casing lay open, top flung back and guts exposed. The engine was an older one, full of wires and gears instead of a simple cavitation engine that would accelerate the water flowing through it to huge speeds. Old or not, it was better than the nothing they'd had before.

At least it wasn't a combustion engine. Narcisse hated digging grease and oil out from under her claws. The smell of the cleaning fluids was bad enough, especially mixed with the rising stink of the ocean and the strangely concentrated salt smell that might, possibly, be related to the aliens that Shani was so worried about.

Maybe.

There'd been the faintest edge of a salt smell in the lava tube when the bugs fled into the deeper darkness. Narcisse had almost convinced herself that it was her imagination, but now the salt smell lingered in the air around the dock even though she saw nothing when she looked over the side of the boat. Clear water or not, there was nothing to be seen.

She was certain something was there despite that.

"I can't believe they have such an old boat in a luxury house like this," Tracey complained as she hit the power and tested the accelerator.

The boat's engine purred, then roared. Narcisse nodded approvingly. It wasn't what she wanted. What with the drag from the water, they wouldn't go half as fast as Narcisse would have preferred, but it was way better than it had been before she got her hands into the engine's guts.

Just in time, too.

"They're coming!" Payton called as xe ran out of the vacation house with Shani at xyr side.

Xe had weapons at the ready, a short-muzzled needler and a longer blaster that might take out something in a middle distance. Nothing long range, which was so not good when they had flyers coming in at them.

Shani leaped from the shore all the way to the boat at the end of the dock, digging her claws into its water-worn wood to keep from going all the way into the ocean. Narcisse waved for her to get on while watching Payton who looked like xe might just hang back and get xemself killed protecting their retreat.

"Get your butt on this boat!" Narcisse shouted at him at the same time she smelled the people coming out of the jungle on the far side of the house. "Move! They're coming by land, too!"

Payton ran for it, barely diving onto the boat as Tracey and Shani unmoored the boat and then dropped the engine into the water so that they could go. The punch of speed as Tracey gunned the engine was sharp enough that Payton nearly slid right out of the boat. Narcisse grabbed at xem and wrestled xem into a seat.

The people who emerged from the jungle looked like Payton. They had very similar uniforms, very similarly androgenous builds. The weapons they carried looked much the same, too, except some of them had longer blasters that looked like rifles.

"Go!" Narcisse shouted at Tracey.

"Going!"

The nearest island was off to the east, straight towards the rising sun. The volcano at the center of the island silhouetted against the sun seemed more like a paper cutout than a real island. It was so very far away.

Tracey turned south, heading towards the lava flows that plunged into the sea. Narcisse would've cursed at Tracey for it if the sudden dodge hadn't gotten them out of the way of a barrage of blaster fire aimed directly east.

Payton whirled and pointed xyr longer blaster back at the shore, firing three quick bursts. Three attackers fell. The others scrambled for cover, which gave Tracey just enough time to get them away from the medium range blaster's fire. It did nothing whatsoever for the flyers zooming down at them from the volcano at the center of the island.

"This isn't going to work!" Narcisse shouted.

It couldn't. Calculations ran through Narcisse's head as she considered the speed of their stolen boat, the speed of the flyers and the sheer number of attackers rolling up to their feet to shoot at them again.

"Take this," Payton said, thrusting xyr blaster into Narcisse's hands. "Try to ration your shots."

"I wish I had a damned rifle!" Narcisse complained. "I'm so much better with them than these things."

She did her best, of course, but she was nowhere near as accurate as Payton who'd gotten a perfect score with xyr three shots. When Narcisse fired, careful and measured and as steady as she could be given how Tracey fishtailed the boat to keep the attackers from locking on and blowing their heads off, Narcisse only got two out of her five shots.

Horribly bad. Mother would be looking at Narcisse with one hand over her mouth and raging disappointment in her eyes. Her aunties would all be clucking like hens over how bad Narcisse's aim had gotten in her cushy job.

Next to Narcisse, Payton pulled out bits and pieces of equipment that xe clicked together into a long bar. Then xe took the blaster back and attached the bar to the tip of it. A few more bits turned the butt into a proper rifle mount that you could stabilize against your shoulder. Narcisse gasped, snatching back the blaster that had been converted into a darling little sniper rifle.

"I love it!" Narcisse exclaimed.

"Ah..." Payton started to say only to snap xyr mouth shut as Narcisse set the blaster properly on her shoulder.

The first shot took the lead attacker down. Her second and third shots got the ones with rifles. The fifth shot got the guy on a comm calling for help to kill them all. Then Narcisse turned and aimed up at the flyer that was stooping out of the sun on their boat.

This time the first shot just dented the screen. The second went through and the third, aimed directly at one of the engine pods, blew the thing out of the sky.

"You had a sniper rifle this whole time and didn't tell us?" Tracey complained as she turned the boat back towards the closest island. "What the hell?"

"Components to turn my blaster into a rifle," Payton corrected, "but it won't last for long. Twenty-five shots at most."

"Thank you for telling me that before I blew the thing up in my face," Narcisse said with no hint of sarcasm at all. "Punch it, Tracey."

"Please!" Shani squeaked.

Honestly squeaked, voice coming out far too high for such a large creature. Her tail-hand was clamped onto one of the seat legs and her claws had dug into the floor so deeply that Payton almost expected to see water spurting up, as if the floor was the base of the boat. Shani's eyes were like saucers as she stared at the water swirling in front of the boat.

There was a circle of water widening in front of them that boiled. If a volcano had erupted directly out of it, Narcisse wouldn't have been surprised. Except that no, it wasn't a volcano. There were no fumes, no red glow, just bubbles roiling the water and the rising scent of concentrated salt.

More streams of violent bubbling zoomed in at the circle. No, at them. It was so very much like watching a torpedo at full speed that Narcisse started counting down to impact in the back of her mind. The bubble streams turned away.

They turned away and swooped around the circle, then whooshed past the boat at speeds that made Narcisse's heart leap right up into her throat. How fast could the aliens go?

"Avoid that!" Payton snapped at Tracey.

"Supercavitation," Narcisse noted in a far too clinical voice. "Well, I'd say that confirms the underwater alien theory."

"Crap." Tracey spun the wheel and punched the boat's engines up to full speed.

They jerked up into a hydroplane over the water's surface, skipping along so fast that Payton hooked xyr toes under the seat in front of xem so that xe wouldn't skid right out of the boat. Narcisse barely paid attention, far more focused on a pair of flyers coming in from the north and a third flyer coming from the south.

"What range does this have?" Narcisse asked.

"Maximum is five kilometers," Payton said, "but you won't be able to punch through armor at that range. It would take repeated shots."

"Great."

Narcisse looked at the boiling trails of water streaming alongside the boat as if considering firing on these mystery aliens. It wouldn't do a bit of good. The blaster's beam would refract on the water's surface. Even a proper projectile like Payton's needler wouldn't be effective. Hitting the water's surface tension would dramatically decelerate the needle and keep it from hurting anyone. She was pretty sure the explosive needles wouldn't arm properly in water, too. At best they would fragment on the surface and become useless bits of slowly drifting downwards shrapnel.

"Don't," Shani warned.

"No, I wasn't going to," Narcisse said. "I was just wishing I had ammonia. Or bleach. Big old barrel of it. A tanker, maybe. Fill the bay with so much that it kills everything in the water."

Shani's tail tried to curl into a corkscrew as her sides shook with sudden laughter, but her grip on the seat leg didn't allow much curling at all. "Wouldn't do much good."

"Sulfur?" Narcisse suggested, eyes locked on the approaching flyers and tone light.

"Nope. Lava isn't a problem."

"Pity," Narcisse complained. "Well, I suppose if I had a big enough supply of sulfur dioxide then it wouldn't matter either way."

Shani turned to stare at Narcisse, ears back against her skull. "You're going to strip the oxygen out of the water entirely."

"Well, I would," Narcisse said. "I mean, if I had the means to do it, but of course I don't right now. I do imagine it would do rather nasty things to any sea creatures, though."

The boiling trails of water veered wider away from the path of the boat. Narcisse blinked and nodded. Well, that was nice. It was possible to threaten this alien species convincingly.

That she absolutely would attempt to kill them if given the chance was irrelevant at the moment. Hopefully, she'd get the chance to do it properly sometime soon, once she had some good chemical resources to work with.

Hopefully.

Had to survive to the next island, first.

Either way, the south flyer swooped down at them. Narcisse took aim and punched a hole straight through the left engine pod. The flyer screamed into the ocean, spiraling and leaving a corkscrew trail of flame and smoke.

No one ejected.

The other two flyers from the north pulled up and away, heading back up the coast. That made Narcisse grit her teeth. As glad as she was not to be gunned down from above, it only meant that they would be attacked as soon as they got in range of the other island. She couldn't imagine just what stories were going out over the comms about the four of them.

"Any comms?" Narcisse asked as she scanned the skies for any more flyers and kept an eye on the escort of supercavitating aliens around the boat.

"Only into space," Payton said far too grimly. "I don't know that it will help. For all I know, the attackers were sent by the ship to take us out."

"No," Shani said. "They're not from the ship. They're local."

"You're sure?" Narcisse asked.

"Quite," Shani said.

She'd crouched down in the well of the boat, so low that her head and shoulders were below the railing. It was as if Shani had decided that if the sea aliens couldn't see her, then she was safe. Or maybe she was trying to hide from them as much as possible.

Narcisse honestly wasn't sure. The stink of the salt was so strong that it hurt her nose. Shani's nose had to be killing her. Worse, the circle of bubbles chased after them like a predator tracking its prey over an open field.

"Don't hesitate to destroy the boat to get us up on land," Narcisse told Tracey.

"Way ahead of you, big sister," Tracey said. Her fingers were white on the steering wheel. "You should all be ready to jump because when we get close to land is when things are going to go deadly."

"Oh, I don't know," Narcisse said, turning back to the rear of the boat to stare at the chasing circle of bubbles. "We're being run to ground, Tracey. They're still pacing us and chasing us."

Tracey glanced behind and then cursed under her breath as she pushed the boat to the maximum speed possible, even though it made the entire boat vibrate worryingly. Narcisse hummed and went back to watching. She only had a few shots left with the rifle. Payton had only the needler.

And Shani was so terrified that her shorn fur stood up on end.

"Get us to the beach, Tracey," Narcisse ordered. "Whatever it takes, get us there."

"I will," Tracey promised just as grimly as she breathed in, breathed out and focused fully on the driving, claws flexed out and quietly dripping venom against the steering wheel.

Narcisse nodded.

Let the aliens come. Whatever happened, they had their venom and Narcisse would not lose this fight no matter what.

FOURTEEN
FLASHING CLAWS SPITTING VENOM

FUCK, boats were horrible. Payton gritted xyr teeth as they whipped across the surface of the waves. Why couldn't this thing have wings? Flying so was much better than this water-bound skipping and bouncing across the waves.

Every wave smacked into the boat's hull like a blow to the breastbone, vibrating it like they were riding in an out of tune bell instead of a proper vehicle. The wind whipped sounds away, so it was impossible to hear a flyer coming at them. Payton scanned the skies all around but xe didn't think xe would see a flyer coming at them.

They were heading straight into the sunrise, blind as if they wore blast helmets, and they had no way to defend themselves at all. Xyr needler was down to one final pack of needles, not even explosive ones. Narcisse's rifle only had two shots left, neither of which was going to do a damn bit of good against whatever the hell was in the water.

"Hold on!"

Tracey's shout came a hair's breadth before she wrenched the wheel and sent them skipping across the waves in a dramatic swerve to the right. Then they careened back to the left, avoiding… something?

Two seconds later, as Payton opened xyr mouth, a whirlpool exploded upwards into a waterspout out of clear skies.

"What the fuck?" Payton gasped.

"Oh," Narcisse said, voice inaudible but mouth perfectly readable, "I guess that's a problem."

More waterspouts formed as Tracey spun and flung the boat back and forth, avoiding whatever warning signs she'd noticed. The next island got closer by the moment, but the waterspouts worked at fencing them in so that they couldn't go that direction.

Tracey's cursing rose over the roar of the waterspouts and the thrum of the engines. "I don't think we can make it."

"Keep going," Narcisse replied, cocking her rifle and aiming over Tracey's head. "Payton, Shani, don't let me fall out of the boat."

Payton holstered xyr needler, hooked xyr ankles under the seat's bolted legs, and then grabbed Narcisse around the waist. Shani's tail snaked around Payton's waist and then grabbed onto Narcisse's thigh.

For a long, endless few seconds that felt like a decade, Narcisse stood in the back of the boat and aimed her rifle towards the bow of the boat. Then, as Tracey gasped and a trio of waterspouts formed directly in front of them far too close for them to dodge, Narcisse fired right at the base of the middle waterspout.

The rifle blast blew a hole through the waterspout.

A small one.

But big enough that Tracey shouted in triumph as she drove the boat straight through the gap. It closed around the boat, around Narcisse whose rifle ripped out of her hands as the water tried to drag her away from Payton and Shani.

Payton held xyr breath and hung one. Shani's tail was a steel band around Payton's waist. The water clawed at xem, battering xyr arms and hands, gouging at xyr eyes, nose and mouth.

Then they were through, water spraying everywhere.

"Get ready to jump!" Tracey shouted.

Payton shook the water out of xyr eyes, arms still locked around Narcisse's waist. Xe tensed as the shore rushed at them, sandy dunes and pale green and lavender sea grass approaching so fast that xe felt like xe'd been shot out of a cannon.

Shani whined, high and loud enough that it made Narcisse shudder.

"Keep gunning it!" Narcisse shouted to Tracey. "The water's coming up with us, Tracey!"

"Of fucking course it is," Tracey complained. "Right. Fine. Let's fucking do this, then."

It took a moment for Payton to realize what Narcisse meant. The sand rushed at them but the waves under the boat didn't break. They didn't curl and collapse into chaotic fractal patterns of foam and bubbles.

Instead, the waves cupped the boat and sucked at it. Pulled it back towards the open ocean despite the way Tracey gunned the engines. Payton hauled Narcisse down into the well of the boat, shoving her down next to Shani who whined and growled expletives that Payton recognized but didn't understand.

"We're down," Payton shouted to Tracey as xe draped xemself over both Narcisse and Shani, clinging to the seat legs to form a living seat-belt for the most important people in the boat.

"Good!"

Tracey whipped the boat around so hard and fast that Payton's zero-G training kicked in. Xe sucked in a breath, locked their eyes on Narcisse's abruptly clammy face, and grit xyr teeth against the surge of vertigo.

Then they whipped back in the other direction, still so fast that it felt like asteroid destroyer duty, riding in a tiny fighter and blasting asteroids before they could threaten xyr home space station. The boat groaned, sides shuddering as the waves and the engines fought each other. Tracey howled with outrage and cut to the left in a whirl that had to be uncontrolled.

Water fountained around them. There were dark shapes in the water, long and lean with tentacles. Payton's eyes crossed as xe tried to make out who or what they were. Pain stabbed through xyr head as lilting, bubbling voices surged through xyr mind.

"Oh, that's just rude," Narcisse observed far too calmly for the way Tracey swore, the way Shani whined. Or for the way Payton moaned in agony. "How very dare you?"

Xe shut xyr eyes. Grit xyr teeth. And gasped as they suddenly lanced forward.

"Ha!" Tracey shouted. "Impact!"

Pretty much the instant she shouted it, the boat rang like a gong. Payton lost xyr grip on the seat legs. It didn't matter. Narcisse had her arms around Payton's waist. Shani leaped so high and so far that she looked like gravity no longer existed for her.

As the sky went grey and the surging ocean water scrabbled at the boat, Narcisse threw Payton over her shoulder and leaped from the boat. Tracey leaped with her. They ran like Shani, like the predators they were, dashing through the sand and pastel sea grass away from the ocean and the tentacled aliens hiding under the surface.

By the time they reached solid ground a dozen meters away, Payton's head cleared. Xe looked across the water for boats. Nothing. Then up at the sky.

A flyer hung in the sapphire sky, frozen in one instant of time in a swooping bank towards them. Sunrise glinted off the forward-facing cannons. Xe had one instant of glimpsing faces inside the viewscreen before the golden sunshine turned it into a blinding mirror.

"Incoming!" Payton bellowed.

Xe twisted in Narcisse's arms to break free. She dropped xem and then hauled xem back up to xyr feet when xe stumbled. Then they all ran for the looming trees that climbed the steep slope beyond the shore.

Steep slope, easily thirty degrees. Mix of fern trees with their lacy branches and spiky things that would stab at them. Needler, no explosive needles, no rifle. No other weapons.

Payton ran as hard as xe could for the tree line. Shani had already disappeared into the underbrush. Narcisse ran at xyr side. Tracey loped ahead of them, arms and legs moving so smoothly that you'd have thought she was jogging on a track, not running for her life.

"Cave!" Payton shouted.

"None close!" Tracey shouted back. "Shani's on something. Hurry!"

The cannons started firing behind them. Sand sprayed up into the sky. Then pastel sea grass. Then the spikey fronds tore at Payton's cheeks. One clipped the corner of xyr eye, cutting it open for an instant. The wound closed instantly.

No blood fell on the ground. Just cannon blast that tore through the brush and shrubs and fern-trees as if they weren't there.

The whine of a ground-based cannon thrumming into life sounded in front of them. Payton gasped and ran harder. Cannon, cannon, thank fuck for a cannon!

It was well-shielded, with a force field that Tracey opened for the two of them. The body of it was armored steel with plascrete reinforcement overtop. Payton dove into it, shoving Shani away from the controls. She'd managed to power the thing up, thank fuck, but her stubby toe-fingers and tail-hand couldn't operate the controls properly.

"Let's see how you like it," Payton snarled as xe started firing without bothering to target the flyer.

Three shots and the targeting computer finally booted up. Payton lined up the cannon and fired.

The flyer bloomed into an explosion that rocked them all. Payton blew out a breath before slapping both Narcisse and Tracey away from the controls. Three more flyers in-coming. The cannon, darling wonderful thing that it was, had long-range ammo. Three shots, three kills.

Payton nodded approvingly as xe scanned the skies, the neighboring islands and then flipped the comms on.

"Mayday! This is Payton Wu requesting immediate backup from any Gensyn in the area. Drath under attack by alien species, unknown. Local forces are compromised, potentially mind-controlled. Strict environmental control necessary. Urgent, urgent, do not engage with the water. Alien species can control waterspouts."

Xe sucked in a breath to babble the whole thing again but the comm system screeched and then blew up.

"Fuck, they really are powerful, aren't they?" Payton complained as xe brushed off the bits of shrapnel that had pierced xyr face. "Fucking fine. At least that got out. Any weapons?"

Narcisse and Tracey, like the sensible predators they were, had already ransacked the cannon's interior. Tracey grinned over her new rife-blaster while Narcisse looked unutterably smug about her hand-held blasters, two of them, and the stack of blasters, needlers and grenades that she'd amassed for Payton.

"Oh, that's beautiful," Payton crooned as xe set to work loading every single one of them onto xyr body. "Come to mama, darlings."

Thank fuck Payton still had xyr uniform on. Xe had all the attachment points, pockets and clips needed to take every single one of them without issue. It'd be a little tight on ammo, but Narcisse was busily loading spare ammo clips onto belts that someone had kindly left behind in their ammo locker.

Adjustable ones, how nice. They could all carry them, even Shani. Payton nodded for Tracey to grab a couple, then smiled as Shani and Narcisse followed suit with belts full of enough ammo to start a small war.

Narcisse blinked as she loaded more belts for Payton. "...Was your mother especially violent?"

"Fuck yes," Payton agreed with a big grin. The last needler went into one of xyr shoulder pockets and then xe strapped on belts of ammo while grinning at Narcisse. "Ma was the one who taught me how to fight, shoot and kill. Pa took care of the kids while Ba handled all the computers and scanners and like. My other parents had different skills, some overlapping, but Ma was the warrior and damn good at it, too."

"Humans are so odd," Shani murmured. "There are more humans coming, you know."

"Well, of course," Payton said. "Any transport in the area? Preferably not water-based."

Xe stood and bounced on xyr toes a little bit to make sure xe had everything settled securely. A couple of the blasters needed to be shifted around so that they wouldn't swing and throw xyr stride off but for the most part xe had a good arrangement.

Training did make a difference.

"Not that I can smell," Shani said as Narcisse and Tracey both shook their heads.

"Right, then we kill our way through the attackers and steal their transport," Payton said. "Any issues with that? Any injuries?"

"Just your eye," Narcisse said. "And face?"

"It's healed," Payton said, brushing off the concerned look Shani gave him. "Barely even felt it."

Which was true, though non-Gensyn never understood that xe meant it when xe claimed an injury hadn't hurt. Frankly, papercuts hurt worse than getting an eye put out or needles through xyr body. They healed slower, after all.

"All right," Payton said as xe charged the smallest blaster up. "This will be bloody. I wouldn't be at all surprised if those water aliens actually were controlling people."

"They tried with us," Narcisse said. She shrugged. "It was terribly rude the things they said. Odd grammar, too."

"...Right," Payton said. "Well, don't be surprised if the attackers behave weirdly. Just kill them, get them out of our way, and duck if I yell that I'm throwing a grenade."

Xe didn't really remember any words from the sea aliens, just pain in xyr head and disorientation so bad that xe wanted to pass out. Whoever these new, unknown aliens were, Payton had them on xyr shit-list now. They had to be part of why everything had gone so wrong on this mission so far.

Actually, they were probably *all* of why it had gone wrong.

Shani's ears slid back as she leveled devastating puppy eyes on Payton.

Yeah, it was them. Xe already knew that Shani couldn't talk about them for whatever reason. One of the things that Ma had always wondered about was why none of the other alien species ever came to meet humanity. They existed. The Drath admitted it openly. Six other races of aliens lived in the greater galaxy, none of them strong enough to challenge the Drath's absolute rule.

Except maybe that wasn't true.

Maybe this was the start of a war between alien species with humans as pawns in a battle between powers and technologies that none of them could comprehend.

Shani winced as her tail curled under her belly. Narcisse winced as well, rubbing her hand over Shani's head and down her neck. The misery in Shani's drooping ears and her tucked tail told epics about just how close the margin between the Drath and these sea aliens was.

With humanity trapped between them.

Well, that was that.

Payton took a breath, nodded to the other three, and then threw open the door of the cannon so that they could continue the battle to freedom. Because Gensyn were nothing if not determined to live no matter what the odds, and Narcisse and Tracey looked like they were much the same.

Those aliens were going to find out why humanity was the supreme lifeform in every single solar system they'd colonized.

FIFTEEN
AGAINST POWERS UNSEEN

THE MORNING AIR stank of fear and sea salt as they stepped outside. Narcisse let the fear fill her lungs. Her claws flexed out instinctively. Fear meant prey. Prey meant predators, bigger ones that Narcisse and Tracey, fiercer ones that Shani. And if the bigger predators were coming, well, that meant that Narcisse had to be that much faster, that much more focused, that much more deadly.

Huh. Her venom was going to be absolutely vicious for a while, wasn't it?

So be it.

The salt scent tasted far too complex for actual sea salt. The cephalopodic aliens chattered away in the background of Narcisse's mind, fracturing her understanding of grammar as they muttered threats against Shani.

They didn't seem to notice Narcisse at all.

No, that was inaccurate. They noticed. But only in the way that Narcisse would notice a beetle or a mouse. Not like a person. An animal in the environment that could be discounted unless it suddenly behaved strangely. Then she, and every other human, would be squished like a bug.

Shani flinched.

Ah. So that was what was going on. Not only was this an attack, a revolution against the Drath starting in one small, unimportant place, it was also something that could very well destroy the entirety of the human race.

Because if the cephalopodic aliens could destroy humans here, if the Drath couldn't and didn't bother stopping it, then they could and would destroy humans everywhere.

"You can't..." Shani murmured to Narcisse as Tracey and Payton headed out of the cannon, weapons at the ready.

"Shani, humans fight to defend themselves," Narcisse said entirely calmly. "That's just the way we are. We adapt, and we fight, and we kill as we have to. Those aliens don't understand what they're dealing with. They think that they're far above us, as you are, but that's not necessarily true. Still, just because I understand their point of view doesn't mean that I'll go blabbing about it to everyone. Let's go. We have killing to do and an escape to make happen somehow."

Shani wheezed a grim soundless laugh, tail tucked under her belly instead of curled into loops. "Somehow."

"Didn't I say we adapt?" Narcisse said with a quick grin that knocked Shani's ears back. "We'll figure it out. Let's go!"

Narcisse ran out after Tracey and Payton, following Tracey's jittery scent of anticipation and Payton's dead-calm certainty that xe was unkillable, unstoppable, and pissed right off. Seriously, the attackers didn't know what they had coming at them. And neither did the cephalopodic aliens.

The shrubbery around the cannon installment was thick enough to shield the attackers from Narcisse's eyes. It did nothing whatsoever to hide their scents. Tracey was in the lead with Payton on her heels. The two of them smelled focused, deadly, ready to deal death against everyone coming their way.

Narcisse breathed in the salty air and nodded as she caught the wafting scent of attackers sneaking up on the left, creeping along the edge of the tree line in an attempt to get at their backs. When Narcisse nodded that way, Shani blew out a breath and jerked her head as she snapped hard in their direction.

Her scent agreed that death was the only choice.

They ran together through the ferns and palms, louder than Narcisse preferred as they went through the plants, but the attackers seemed to be nose-blind and ear-deaf because they didn't react at all until Shani leaped straight at the throat of the first one.

Teeth gaping.

One snap, a spray of blood and the first attacker went down dead. Narcisse leaped after Shani; claws extended. A few quick scratches has their very baseline human attackers dropping to the lavender grass with foam boiling up out of their mouths. In a matter of moments, the circling attackers lay dead, half from Narcisse's poison, half from Shani's teeth and claws.

"Back," Narcisse said, already heading back up the hill towards Tracey and Payton.

Shani hesitated, staring out to sea with her ears slapped against her skull. She ran in place as if afraid to turn her back on the ocean. Narcisse hummed and looked out to sea. The ever-shifting song of the sea aliens suddenly went into sharps and flats of discordant surprise.

"She's mine," Narcisse announced to the sea aliens. "I will protect her."

The surf surged out towards sea, exposing the sand in a rush that was as sharp as any tsunami. Narcisse's breath caught. Oh. Goodness, that was a tsunami. One manufactured by the aliens but it would be just as deadly as a natural one.

This time Shani leaped into a run without Narcisse saying a word. They barreled through the forest without bothering to hide their passage. Honestly, they probably sounded like flyer crashing into the hillside.

"Tsunami!" Narcisse bellowed as they caught up to the pitched battle between Payton and their set of attackers.

"Fucking hell!" Payton yelled back in a high-pitched squawk of dismay. "Duck!"

Xe flung not one grenade but three, unerringly landing them in the middle of their attackers. Narcisse didn't bother ducking. She kept running towards the steep mountainside behind their attackers. Tracey and Shani were on her heels.

The grenades went off at Narcisse's back. Three quick blaster shots and then Payton charged after them, cursing the whole way. Apparently, Payton left some attackers alive because there were a couple of other people cursing, too.

Their voices disappeared in the rumble of far too much water coming up the shore. And then up the hillside. The tsunami roared like a hungry lizard back home, one of the big ones that could eat a human in a single bite. Narcisse kept running, leaping up the hillside, scrambling for hand holds and foot holds in the probably vain hope that they could get away from the generated tsunami before it ran out of energy.

"Won't!" Shani barked.

"Fuck," Tracey gasped and then darted ahead of Narcisse. "Transport ahead!"

Narcisse glanced back and nearly screamed at the sight of huge fern trees and spiky palms toppling under a churning wave of debris-filled water. The ocean's water had been stunningly clear. This wave was black with sand, muck and debris.

They would not survive if they got caught by that wave.

Narcisse grabbed Payton who was just barely keeping up. Xe didn't protest when Narcisse threw Payton over her shoulder. Xe just hung on, cursing under xyr breath and grunting for each leaping step Narcisse took.

There was a road ahead, halfway up the hill. Cut into the mountainside with raw yellow-orange verges and a hard-packed yellow-brown crushed stone surface. It stood out, stark against the verdant greens.

On the road sat a hovercar. A single soldier stood by the hovercar, eyes wide and mouth opened as he stared down the hillside towards the roiling tsunami chasing them up the mountain. Tracey charged straight at him.

He dropped; neck broken. Shani leaped into the back of the hovercar. Narcisse tossed Payton in and then jumped into the passenger side while Tracey leaped straight over her head into the driver's seat.

Tracey slapped the controls, kicked the hovercar into life, and then shoved them forward so sharply that Narcisse nearly fell out despite expecting it. Shani kept Payton in the hovercar. Both Narcisse and Shani's claws punched screeching holes into the frame of the hovercar.

"How far can they chase us?" Tracey demanded as she took the rough mountain road higher and higher, looping up the hillside towards the summit where they would run out of places to go.

"As far as they want," Shani replied entirely too fatalistically.

"Hm." Narcisse studied the wave, clinging to her seat while staring over her shoulder. "Can they?"

"What?" Payton asked as xe squirmed around. "Fuck but that's terrifying. What the hell? How are they doing that?"

"Water is their element," Narcisse observed thoughtfully. She rocked and then leaned into the curve as Tracey hauled the wheel and took them up a side road that went up a thirty-degree slope. "They control it utterly. But. Shani. Are they an open-water species or a estuary species?"

Shani stared at Narcisse, blinking rapidly. Her ears hadn't risen off her skull yet, but she still frowned and then shook hard enough to send a cloud of hair and dander up behind them.

"Clear water," Shani said. "Their babies grow in estuaries but only if there's clear, flowing water."

"Ah, good," Narcisse said with a smile that felt utterly smug. "They won't be able to keep this up forever, then. We just have to stay ahead of them until they have to stop and breathe."

The cursing from Payton creatively implied that Narcisse's brains had been radiation blasted to the point where she couldn't figure out how to piss in a pot even with video instructions and a professional personal care attendant.

The cursing from the sea aliens was angry, desperate.

Young.

They sounded young. Rash. Like insulted teenagers or very young adults who had too much pride to admit that they might have made a mistake. Which this surely was.

The farther the tsunami chased them, the more debris it picked up. Where it had been murky green at the seashore, smokey as they fled up the hill, now it was black as night and turning into a mudslide that refused to allow gravity to stop its aspirations.

Narcisse smiled and watched as the wave thickened, no longer churning so much as lurching up the hillside. As Tracey flung them around another corner, up another thirty-five-degree road that climbed towards the volcanic summit of this island, the wave began to crack and grumble.

"What the hell?" Payton asked.

"Not enough water, too much debris," Narcisse said with amusement. "Yes, they can keep following us, but they have to stop to drop the debris, or they need more water to do it. They need to stop to breathe."

And when they did, it was as abrupt as a winded runner stumbling to a stop, hands on their knees as they wheezed for air.

The tsunami tumbled to a stop. Debris precipitated out of it so quickly that it looked like an alien vessel materializing out of the raw soil. Then the water formed up into six bubbles that were about the same size as the hovercar.

At the center of each, Narcisse could see a single cephalopodic alien. Their tentacles waved threateningly at Narcisse. She smiled at them and pictured herself hugging Shani around the neck. Laying claim.

They were high enough, now, for Narcisse to see the moment when a waterspout two kilometers across formed in the ocean. All six of the alien bubbles of water rippled and bounced guiltily. A weird harmonic hummed through Narcisse's mind.

It felt of exasperation, of a mother looking at her troublesome children who'd made a huge mess, of those heart-stopping few moments right before you got the lecture that you so deserved.

The bubbles flattened a bit and then, bless them, they turned and skimmed back down the mountain.

Away from Narcisse, Tracey, and Payton.

Away from Shani.

Narcisse blew out a breath, heart abruptly pounding as she realized just how close that could have been. If the commander had sent them onwards, if the young attacking cephalopods had chosen to ignore the order to return, they wouldn't have escaped.

But they did.

"Find us a comm," Narcisse told Tracey. "A comm or some way to get to the mainland. We can't keep fighting this way for much longer."

"On it," Tracey promised. "It's going to be a challenge, but I'm on it."

Tracey slowed down enough that Narcisse didn't have to cling to the seat anymore. While Payton checked all of xyr armor and weapons, Shani crept forward enough that she could put her head in Narcisse's lap.

Narcisse pet her, smoothing her hand over those velvet-soft ears that wouldn't rise from Shani's skull.

"I won't let them take you," Narcisse promised in a murmur too quietly for anyone, even Shani to hear it. She trusted Shani's nose to pick it up even with the wind blowing their scents away.

Shani pressed her head against Narcisse's belly and didn't reply.

SIXTEEN
FOR FEAR OF CONSEQUENCES UNTOLD

THE ONLY NICE thing about being at the top of a volcano in the middle of an island at the heart of the southern ocean was that it had a spectacular observatory at the top. Well shielded, both from the high mountain air and the stray bits of lava that the volcano threw up every from months. It was a block of heavily armored plasteel with force fields covering it, bare, ugly and utilitarian.

With the most beautiful comm system Payton had ever seen.

"Fuck yes, finally," Payton crooned as xe turned the thing on and set to calling for help on every single band that xe could get.

Given how powerful the comm system was, Payton got replies from every single ship in orbit, the mainland who were startled to have a Gensyn alert coming through their land-based comm system, and a Drath vessel that was who knew where.

"Mayday, mayday," Payton called as Narcisse and Tracey shoved ration bars hidden away in one drawer into their mouths and Shani shivered in the middle of the room like she was afraid to touch anything. "This is Gensyn Payton Wu, guarding Drath Shani. We are under attack by sea-based aliens."

"Cephalopodic," Narcisse interrupted. "Squid-like."

"Configuration is squid-like cephalopods," Payton continued with a nod to Narcisse. "Mind-control effects on humans in the area have been experienced and repelled with difficulty. They control weather and water to the point of waterspouts and whirlpools on command. We were chased halfway up the volcano by a tsunami before the attacking strike team was called back. Urgent assistance needed!"

"Gensyn Wu," a growling Drath said over the comms, cutting off the responding calls from everyone else. "Did you have visual confirmation of the Women of the Sea?"

"Yes," Payton said. "I personally sighted six individuals during the tsunami attack and at least one attacked my mind previously. Poison of some sort was used against Drath Shani. We had to shave her fur to save her life."

The growling bark that answered that was so shocked that Payton glanced over at Shani who'd flopped down on her belly with her paws over her nose and her tail-hand covering her eyes. Narcisse huffed a laugh and petted Shani, eyes laughing even though she didn't make a sound.

"We will be there shortly," the Drath on the comms said. "Are you in a safe place?"

"Hell no!" Tracey shouted from the doorway. "We have incoming!"

"Attackers incoming," Payton said. "Leaving the channel open but we'll be heading for the mainland by any means necessary. Shut the, whatever you called them, the Women of the Sea down and we'll get Shani home no matter who among the locals tries to stop us."

"Done," the Drath on the comms growled. They growl-barked something that made Shani scramble back to her feet.

"We need to hurry," Shani said, not even bothering to reply. "This is getting so out of hand."

"You didn't start it," Payton said as xe charged xyr blaster, "and you're not the one escalating it. We just want to get to safety. They're the ones making things worse all the time."

Xe left the comms open and active so that the whole solar system could hear what happened. It wouldn't last, of course. Their attackers probably had orders to shut the comms down. Given the power of the Drath, keeping this quiet was the only way that the Women of the Sea had to keep from being destroyed.

Or at least to keep from being attacked. Payton had spent a good amount of time around the Drath. Xe'd never seen the sort of power the Women of the Sea showed. Laughter, cuddles and snapping mock-fights, yes. This sort of brutal command of the elements and cold-blooded determination to eliminate someone, no.

"How long on reinforcements?" Payton asked as xe scrambled to the doorway, blaster at the ready.

"Too long," Shani replied. "They're not in close orbit."

"Fuck." Payton sighed. "Right. Narcisse, Tracey, get ready to rip faces off. We need another vehicle, preferably one that flies."

"On it," Narcisse promised. "Though I doubt we'll get anything that will go orbital from this lot."

Yeah, no kidding. Payton snorted a grim laugh at that. These ground-pounders probably had no idea what a proper ship looked like. What xe wouldn't give for a fighter from back home. Honestly, at this point, Payton would give up both xyr left nut and xyr left tit for a ship that could get them out of the range of danger.

Shani barked a little laugh, her tail actually looping for the first time all day.

Then a trio of flyers with heavy cannons swooped down out of the sun and laughter was the last thing on anyone's mind. Payton jerked aside as Narcisse fired a blaster rifle and took out the lead flyer. The other two didn't peel off as xe expected.

They dove in as if they were going to crash straight into the observatory. Payton pushed in and fired xyr blaster on the narrowest beam. That punched through the viewscreen of the left flyer, sending it spiraling to the right. It's wing clipped the right flyer, sending it careening.

Not that it mattered when both Tracey and Narcisse fired right at it and blew up both engines.

"We needed one of those," Payton complained.

"No, we need something that we can use," Narcisse replied. "Those are drones. Nowhere to sit."

Which…

…Huh. They were. Interesting.

"Maybe the attackers are actually using their brains for thinking," Payton said. Then xe snorted. "No. Not a chance."

"Two more incoming, manned," Shani called. Then she yipped and drove under the control panel, tail-hand slapped over her eyes.

Payton tackled Narcisse and Tracey, shoving their faces into the floor at the same time that xe hid xyr face in Narcisse's shoulder.

The flash of light still seared Payton's eyes.

The explosion that followed the light was so loud that it was a punch to the chest rather than something xyr ears picked up. Xe gasped for air, shook xyr head, and then started cursing soundlessly as the volcano rumbled underneath them.

Between the explosion battering all their ears and the growing roar of the volcano, words were impossible.

It didn't matter. Narcisse pushed back to her feet, eyes wide and wild. She sniffed the air, then her mouth moved in curses that Payton couldn't hear. Shani scrambled to her feet, ears swiveling as if she desperately needed to be able to hear over the roar of the waking volcano and couldn't.

"Fuck!" Tracey mouthed the word clearly enough that Payton nodded.

Xe helped her up, then shoved her towards the door. Flyer or not, they needed to get off of the volcano.

Outside the observatory, gravel skittered across the bucking road. The blast of light had, apparently, been some sort of space bombardment weapon. There was a huge column of steam and smoke coming from the ocean between the islands, rising in a mushroom plume that set Payton's heart racing.

Three flyers lay tossed to the ground on the rocky soil near the observatory. Two had crashed badly. One had landed right-side up and more or less intact. It wasn't a long-distance flyer, certainly not orbital, but it would get them down to the coast where they could take over a bigger ship or a better flyer.

Payton charged at the people stumbling out of the intact flyer. One died before he even had a chance to notice Payton was there. The second had time for his eyes to go wide. Then the third went down foaming at the mouth as Tracey clawed his face and flung him aside.

The four of them charged into the flyer, Tracey once again taking the controls. Payton searched the flyer's two rooms, a toilet and a seating area for passengers. No one else. Good.

Narcisse ran back to the controls, sliding into the copilot's chair. Neither she nor Tracey said a word as they powered up and took off so fast that Shani's butt smacked into the floor and Payton went to one knee from the surge of acceleration.

"Where to?" Narcisse called back.

"Far side of the island," Shani replied. "There's a port there with big boats, ones that go way out of sea. There should be something big enough to get us across the ocean even with the Ladies coming at us."

"Will they, after that?" Payton asked.

Shani grimaced, exposing her long fangs. The expression should have been threatening but her rotating ears and tail tucked under her belly to wrap around her stomach made it nervous instead. Great. Not the answer that Payton wanted, but that seemed to be the way xyr luck was going right now.

"Okay, this thing is damaged," Tracey announced as Payton made it into one of the passenger seats. "We're gonna land hard, at best. We might crash outright."

"I'll survive it," Payton promised. "What can we do to protect you, Shani?"

"I'll be fine," Shani yipped with a horrified stare at Payton. "My nanites are even better than yours."

"Good, except no, they're not," Payton said. Xe wagged a finger at Shani that made her growl at xem. "I'm not the one who had squid-bots attacking me through my fur. You're still not back to full normal and I know it."

"You're really not," Narcisse said in the mildest tone of voice ever, especially for someone battling with controls that had Tracey cursing quietly under her breath.

There wasn't much time to consider it. Payton peered through the viewscreen and bit xyr lip. They were coming in far too fast, especially with the possibility of more attacks on landing. Xe grabbed at one of the life vests that were under each seat in case of water landings. They had automatic inflation systems, so Payton blew one up, tossed it to

Shani, then grabbed two more. Shani got one around her neck, then held the other two under her belly and between her fore-legs.

No more time.

As Tracey hauled on the controls, dragging them up, the engines spluttered and then gave out. The flyer dropped like the brick it was shaped like. Payton balled xemself up and let the impact rock xem whatever way it would.

Impact forward. Left and then a sharp right side impact. Payton bounced and fell to the floor, panting.

As the flyer ticked and creaked around them, Payton shook off the impacts and hauled xemself upright. They'd landed upside down, somehow, so the door was wedged shut. Narcisse groaned, caught in the harness in the copilot's seat. Tracey was on the ceiling, shaking her head.

Shani, thankfully, had barely moved, though she did have a bit of blood coming out of her nose.

"Smacked my snout against the floor," Shani said. She snorted, shook her head, and got up, leaving the life vest behind.

"Oof!"

Payton nearly fired but it was only Narcisse landing next to Tracey after releasing herself from the harness. Xe blew out a breath and then tried to open the side door. Nothing. It was wedged shut. Or maybe bent too much to open ever again.

"Fine," Payton snarled.

The butt of a rifle did a lovely job of breaking the already fractured viewscreen. It tumbled out of its frame, giving them a perfect way out of the overturned flyer.

Outside, the streets were chaos. People ran every direction, screaming and terrified. The mushroom cloud loomed higher and higher into the sky. Payton could just see the marina up the street from where they'd landed. It was chaos, too, full of people streaming away from the sea and up towards the shaking volcano.

What a choice. Ride out the inevitable tsunami on a ship that was sure to be dashed to pieces or climb a volcano about to blow. Payton shook xyr head.

"What do we do?" Shani asked.

"The Women of the Sea aren't going to let the ocean kill them," Payton decided after one second of consulting xyr instincts. "The volcano will blow. We go for the marina, find the best, fastest ship we can steal, and then head straight for the mainland."

"It's a plan," Narcisse agreed. "They're still talking. I can still hear them, sort of. They're very, very irritated at the ones who set all this in motion. We might have a chance to get to shore while the Ladies in charge scold the ones who overstepped their authority."

It was a slim chance, but it was the best one Payton had gotten since this whole mess started up.

"I'll take it," Payton decided. "Let's go."

SEVENTEEN
FRIENDS FROM THE FIRST

PANIC HAD such a stink to it. Narcisse had never been able to stand it. Her aversion to the stench of panic was part of why she'd gone into laboratory science rather than anything more adventurous. Why expose herself to something that made her claws flex out and her heart race with sheer rage?

The odd thing Narcisse noted, absently as she raced along at Shani's side, was that the stench of panic sharpened her reflexes. Rather dramatically. Her mind moved faster. Her eyes saw things more clearly. Every sound was clearer, more precise.

And the scents, goodness, the scents were a thousand times more detailed and revealing than she'd ever experienced before.

Narcisse stunned a guard waving her blaster wildly, picked off a blank-faced man who stank of sea salt and the desire to kill, and tracked the scents of the ships they ran past. Good, not fueled up, worn out with grease leaking out of the bearings.

"That one!" Narcisse shouted to Tracey.

"Yeah," Tracey agreed before leaping straight up the gangplank and onto the deck as if she was a velociraptor sighting its prey.

Shani followed suit, joining Tracey in tossing people off the massive yacht and into the water below. Not many of them. Most got tossed over the bow of the yacht onto the deck or the shore, but the few in the water went still and pale before scrambling out to head straight for Payton and Narcisse with blank eyes and fingers clawing at them.

Narcisse stunned all of them.

The Ladies doing the scolding didn't appear to notice that some of their juniors lurked underneath the docks. They definitely didn't notice that the juniors were mind-controlling more people. Narcisse huffed.

"Get on the yacht," Narcisse ordered Payton.

"I'm the—"

Payton snapped xyr mouth shut when Narcisse turned and snarled at xem, fangs in open sight, dripping venom. Xe ran up the gangplank and set to work clearing the lower decks of the yacht. Good. They needed to be sure that the yacht was free of other people. There was no way that anyone could be trusted at this point.

If Chikere and Matija showed up, Narcisse would shoot them in the face. It wouldn't keep them down for very long, but it would make her feel better about their abandonment back on the other island. Narcisse wasn't ever going to forgive that.

"You're very bold to continue your behavior when orbital strikes are already happening," Narcisse commented to the Women of the Sea under the dock. She kept her eyes on the panicking humans running away from the marina. "Even if you survive it, the bad press between all the alien species isn't going to go well."

There was a moment of black annoyance from the three junior Ladies under Narcisse's feet.

Blind-animal-limited cannot comprehend-see-hear truth, one of the Ladies snapped at her.

The words mingled with flaring ribbons of red and neon green in Narcisse's head, mingling with sounds like whale song. The scorn was clear. Such an interesting language, even if it did make Narcisse's head echo and her heart pound against her breastbone like it was trying to escape.

Narcisse could feel layers of intent in the color. The red was anger, sharp as her claws, digging into her brain. The neon green was the intent to kill all humans everywhere. That lingered on Narcisse's tongue like venom gone bitter with rage and disgust. The whale song smelled of dusty old books. Perhaps it was their version of history? That, at least, only made her temples throb instead of smelling like death.

Narcisse hummed and focused on the feeling of hunting through the jungles of home, claws out and ready. Pain was just pain. She could and would ignore it to get the message through. The rich, fetid soil after a rain mingled with the smell of blood and the taste of raw, still-warm flesh on her tongue.

"Fools who go after a species that adapts to every environment they encounter get what they deserve," Narcisse said focusing on all the ways that humanity had conquered every single solar system they'd found, all with technology that was like rubbing two sticks together compared to what the Ladies and the Drath had.

"Narcisse!" Tracey shouted. "Get your butt up here. We have to go!"

"On my way," Narcisse called back. She hummed again and pictured her mother picking her up by the scruff of the neck and shaking her like a doll. "Best to keep hiding, little girls. Your elders aren't pleased with you."

Narcisse leaped up onto the deck instead of taking the gangplank, grabbing the rail with one hand and swinging herself upwards smoothly.

That was a good choice. The Ladies under the dock sent a wave of water up to tear the gangplank away as if that would keep Narcisse from getting on the ship. It wasn't that big, though it was a nicely hefty yacht that would easily hold a party of fifty or more.

It echoed with just the four of them. Narcisse did a quick tour, sniffing the whole way, just to make sure that they were alone on the yacht. They were. The few people who had been here had run from the impending tsunami or been thrown off by Tracey, Shani and Payton. Mostly by Payton, of course.

Xyr furious intent on getting Shani to safety filled the lower decks. Narcisse's shoulders relaxed the more of it she breathed in. By the time she got back up to the deck, Narcisse almost felt like herself.

Other than the angry, frightened, bizarre chatter of the Women of the Sea pounding away in the back of her head, but that was easy enough to ignore. The way her eyes crossed, and her feet stumbled at the louder "shouts" was a bit worrying, though Narcisse pushed that away in favor of getting back to the others.

"Can we pilot this with just the four of us?" Narcisse asked as she followed Tracey's scent into the control center.

"Easily," Tracey said. "Payton's already got the engines up and running. We were just waiting for you, slowpoke."

"Mm, just verifying that we got everyone else off the yacht," Narcisse said. "Let's go. The sooner we're gone, the better."

The junior Ladies burbled angrily. Narcisse felt the moment that they released... something... that felt-smelled like hostile intent. Three seconds later, Payton growled and charged for the door with xyr blaster at the ready.

"Incoming!" Payton shouted. "Get us out of here!"

Xe started firing at the approaching mass of blank-faced dock workers, glazed-eyed guards and random civilians whose jaws japed open like zombies. Narcisse huffed and reached with her mind in a way that she wouldn't have thought she could do until she did it.

"That's rude, girls," Narcisse told the junior Ladies. "You're going to get yourself and your whole species executed if you keep it up."

She made a point of trying to say that to the Women of the Sea further out, the ones cursing in whale song-colored streaks of vermillion rage and neon yellow fear. Her knees went right out from under her as the further out Ladies suddenly noticed her, noticed the juniors, noticed the attack heading straight at their yacht.

"Narcisse?" Shani asked, curling around Narcisse and patting Narcisse's face with her tail-hand. "Don't talk to them! They can fry your brain. Their method of telepathy can cause brain aneurisms."

"That's not good," Narcisse commented against the rising pain in her head. "Am I right that your people will slag the planet rather than let them get away with this?"

Shani flinched. "...Yes."

"Good," Narcisse said. "Because they want to kill all humans. Better to make this planet an example than let them succeed."

She turned her face into Shani's shoulder, burying her face in the short, ragged fur. Shani's rich, complex scent filled Narcisse's sinuses.

It drove out any thoughts of the Ladies and their brain-breaking language. No threat could compare to the joy of cuddling with Shani.

The yacht jerked against the dock and then the engines roared. Oddly, Narcisse didn't feel any movement. She sighed and looked up. They weren't moving, even though Tracey had the controls at full reverse.

"I hope a second strike hits soon," Narcisse said as distinctly as she possibly could. "Right here in the bay."

The junior Ladies under the dock flinched. The senior ones out to sea went neon yellow and purple with emotions that Narcisse didn't try to parse. No point to it. Narcisse didn't want to talk to them at all, not when she had Shani to hug. If there was no other way to get Shani to safety, well, Narcisse would gladly die with her arms wrapped around her soul mate.

"The fuck?" Tracey choked as the engines suddenly shoved the yacht away from shore.

Payton managed, somehow, not to be thrown over the railing even though xe was busy clubbing and blasting attackers so that they couldn't get onto the yacht. Narcisse hummed and smiled as she rubbed her cheek against Shani's shoulder.

"What did you do?" Shani asked in a murmur too quiet for Narcisse to hear it. The question came more from her cinnamon-scented shock than from sounds.

Narcisse smirked and chuckled. "Apparently, I can lie to the Ladies convincingly enough to startle them. At least, I managed it once."

"That was a lie?" Shani asked. Her tail-hand rubbed between Narcisse's shoulder blades.

"Part of it was," Narcisse explained. "I won't let you die. The rest is true enough. I do feel like we were made to be friends, right from the moment we met."

The yacht rocked as Tracey cleared the dock and then spun the wheel. Payton stumbled at the doorway; one eye blackened though the bruise healed as Narcisse stared. Then Tracey punched the engines, and they flew out to sea.

"All right, what the hell was that?" Payton demanded.

"The Women of the Sea have divisions between them," Narcisse explained, head on Shani's shoulder. "I can hear them. And they understand me when I think and speak clearly to them. It's painful, but I can do it."

"She's on the verge of a brain aneurism," Shani said. The gentle rub of her tail-hand between Narcisse's shoulder blades went heavy for a moment.

"But I managed to surprise the rebellious junior Ladies under the dock to let us go," Narcisse explained. "That does absolutely nothing to get us past the ones to sea or to get us back to the mainland, but the Ladies do not like the idea of the planet being slagged."

"I don't like that idea!" Payton exclaimed. "Especially not with us on it!"

Xe sighed and scrubbed a bloody hand over xyr face. There didn't seem to be any cuts or bruises on Payton's knuckles. Must have come from punching people in the face before they left the dock.

"What's the plan?" Tracey asked.

"Straight for the mainland as fast as you can go," Payton said with a grim glare over the water. "Hopefully without waterspouts and whirlpools."

"No guarantees," Narcisse said.

The Ladies, juniors and seniors all, were very not happy about Shani escaping the islands. Their displeasure echoed in Narcisse's aching head. None of the commentary seemed to be directed at Narcisse. She didn't think that Shani heard it either.

"I can't," Shani confirmed in a low murmur. "If I had, I wouldn't have come to the islands. We don't... hear them easily. Most species don't. It's kind of weird that you can."

"Probably a random genetic thing," Narcisse said thoughtfully, or at least as thoughtfully as she could when her head throbbed, and her stomach had gone to knots from the pain. At least she didn't get seasick. That would be horrific on top of the headache.

As the yacht got up to hydroplane speed, the voices of the Ladies shifted and moved away from them. To Narcisse, it felt like they were diving deeper into the ocean, far underneath the surface of the water. Maybe all the way down into the oceanic rifts way out to sea.

Which wasn't exactly a good thing, now was it? Could orbital bombardment kill everything in the deep ocean? She really wasn't sure. Narcisse sighed and pulled herself to her feet with difficulty. She had to lean on Shani's shoulder, but she made it.

"What are you doing?" Payton asked.

"Looking to see what chemicals are available on the yacht," Narcisse said. "I might be able to whip up something nicely toxic to sea life with what's onboard. Possibly. I'll have to check."

Narcisse ignored the disapproving look over Tracey's shoulder, ignored Shani's worried prancing and especially ignored Payton scowl. They weren't to safety yet. Narcisse wasn't going to let the relative quiet time go by without making whatever weapons she could. She had to keep Shani safe, one way or the other.

EIGHTEEN
A HEART TO PINE FOR

WHAT WITH BEING AT SEA, there wasn't much for Payton to do. Xe almost didn't mind it. Almost.

Xyr fingers were still shaking from the adrenaline rush of the final battle. It would've been seriously nice if a few of those creepy civilians had gotten on the boat. Then Payton would've had someone to beat up, throw off the boat, and xe would've felt better.

Instead, there was just checking xyr stolen weapons, counting ammo packs, and frowning at Narcisse as she drifted out of the command center to go do... something.

"Go with her," Tracey ordered.

She didn't take her eyes off the controls, didn't stop scanning the horizon for more waterspouts and whirlpools. Could the sea aliens make whirlpools big enough to sink a boat this big? Payton had to assume that they could. Hell, they'd made a tsunami run straight up the side of the mountain for a terrifyingly long amount of time.

"She needs a keeper?" Payton asked.

"She's got the look," Tracey replied.

And then didn't explain what "the look" was. Payton glowered at her. No response so xe turned to Shani who winced and pranced in place some more.

"She's thinking of making chemical weapons," Shani explained. "And she's... it's weird? Hyper-focused but also kind of not focused at all. I'm very worried about what the Women of the Sea might have done to her brain when she eavesdropped on them."

"Right, I'll keep an eye on her," Payton promised because chemical weapons when you were battle-shocked sounded like the worst idea yet, in the long list of horrible ideas that had happened today.

Was it today? Two days? Three? Payton shook xyr head. This entire trip had blurred together into one undifferentiated mass of fuck-no about three hours into the trip to the islands. Xe wasn't going to call it a new day until they were off this planet and safely away from whatever stupidity the sea aliens were up to.

They were getting off planet. Just like Narcisse was determined to keep Shani safe, Payton was getting off this hell-planet and back to nice, normal space where the only dangers were explosive decompression, normal human assassins, and politics that xe could shoot down instead of having to be nice.

Xe really missed politics back home. What xe wouldn't give for a proper political argument with knives, blasters and someone getting their neck temporarily broken. Things were just simpler when you could stab whatever, or whoever, was bothering you.

"So true," Narcisse murmured.

She'd crawled into a cabinet in the galley, half her body inside of it, half outside. Payton frowned at the bottles and boxes of cleaning chemicals and mold remover that she'd pulled out of it. Most of them had bright cheerful lettering that warned you to keep them away from small children. Presumably you should also keep them away from battle-shocked scientists with venomous claws, but Payton didn't bother.

"I'm not shell-shocked," Narcisse complained, shuffling her knees backwards as she pulled something big and heavy out of the cabinet.

"I still can't believe how accurate your noses are."

"That was out loud, actually," Narcisse said. She wrinkled her nose in a grin as soon as her head came free of the cabinet. "You're muttering."

"Fuck." Payton scrubbed a hand over xyr face. "Lovely. What are you doing? And how dangerous is it to us?"

"I'm taking an inventory of all the lovely chemicals that I can use to kill people with," Narcisse said as she gently set down an alarmingly blazingly red metal can with hazard symbols on the side in neon yellow. "Mostly things that would kill large numbers of sea creatures, of course, but there're supplies here for some amazing chemical bombs. I mean, if I wanted to make chlorine gas, I've got everything I need."

"...No," Payton said once xe got xyr jaw back off the floor. "What the fuck? No! You're dealing with aliens that can control the weather. It's a fucking gas. No chlorine gas. It could blow back on us and even I'd have trouble dealing with that."

"True," Narcisse said far too calmly for Payton's last remaining nerve. "I'm just saying, this yacht has some lovely supplies for bomb-making."

Payton shut his eyes and breathed slowly, deeply, carefully managing xyr rising temper. They were still in danger. Narcisse was deadly. Her venom could easily take Payton down for a while, for too long for it to be an acceptable risk. No shouting and carrying on.

"Still muttering," Narcisse said. She grinned when Payton snapped xyr eyes open to glower at her. "You are. I think you're more shell-shocked than I am."

"Gensyn don't get battle-shock," Payton said. "We get cranky and violent, and then sleep like the dead for a day or two after its all over."

Narcisse nodded as she sorted her plundered chemicals into groups. "That's a good adaption. We tend not to get shell-shock either, though it can happen. I'm honestly not that messed up. A headache, of course, but that's to be expected."

"How bad?" Payton asked.

Xe helped Narcisse carry her chemicals over to the sink where she'd laid out a whole series of pots and pans with measuring cups, spoons and what looked like a glass rod that might once have been used to open and shut blinds.

Back when Payton was a kid, xe'd taken the same lessons everyone else got about improvised weaponry. Xe could make a slingshot that was lethal and xe knew exactly how to make a knife out of virtually anything including plain old plastic.

Narcisse hummed as she measured thirteen different cleaning solutions into secondary containers. "It'd put it about six out of ten, actually. Not enough to stop me, but definitely enough to make me a bit unhappy. You'll probably be happy to hear that the Women of the Sea seem to be pulling away from the shoreline. They've all headed down into the oceanic rift off the coast."

"The one we're going to have to go straight over?" Payton asked with a roll of xyr eyes and a groan that felt like it came from xyr toes.

"No, the one farther out," Narcisse said, laughing under her breath. "That one's just a valley. I mean the actual rift, the one that goes down about four kilometers."

Payton frowned.

If they were going that deep then... they were retreating to their bunker. Every Gensyn station had safe bunkers where the populace could go hide in case of damage to the station, major attacks or civil unrest. There was always some form of civil unrest going on back home.

What it really meant was that the Drath's orbital strike was only the start. The longer they were out on the ocean, the greater the chance was that they were going to get caught in another strike. Worse, the longer they took getting off-world, the more chance there was that the sea aliens were going to counter-attack somehow.

Just how high could they fling water? If they were fully aquatic, they must have gotten to this world somehow. Ships of some sort, presumably. So they had to be able to lift enough water to support their lives out of the gravity well.

Water was heavy.

They had to have a massive amount of power to do that. And that power could certainly be turned to other things if they were at all adaptable. Fuck, they needed to get off this planet.

"We certainly do," Narcisse agreed.

Payton slapped a hand over xyr face. "I am too tired and grumpy for this. Someone's going to die so hard."

"On the other side, hopefully," Narcisse agreed, laughing at xem.

"All right, I have six chemical grenades done. Can we rig up either slingshots to fling them at attackers or timers? I'm not as good with electronics as I am with chemicals."

Payton stared at the six sturdy glass bottles filled with purplish-blue goop. Each of them had a little packet of something white and powdery held with thin plastic and a bit of tape just under the cap. Xe licked their lips and nodded towards the bottles.

"Just how unstable are they?" Payton asked.

"Oh, perfectly stable until the powder joins the liquid," Narcisse said brightly. She clapped her hands and then beamed at xem. "I can take them apart easily enough if I need to, but they'll explode quite nicely if the two mix. The plastic is water soluble, so it will dissolve quite quickly when the gel hits it. A few seconds to a minute later and the chemical reaction will make the whole thing blow. And burn. Quite nicely, actually."

"We'll go with impact," Payton said, a little light-headed at the sheer thought that this woman had created grenades out of cleaning chemicals and some old glass bottles. "Easier, I think."

Whether there would be anyone to throw them at was the question. Payton very carefully helped Narcisse carry her new grenades up to the cockpit, far more cautious with them than she was. The last thing xe wanted was to have one of the things explode in xyr arms.

They were farther out to sea than Payton expected. The islands lay far behind them, distant blue smudges against the horizon. There was a plume of smoke rising from one of the islands with the slowly expanding cloud of the mushroom spreading over the sky like a blanket being laid down over a pile of sleeping children.

Not too far off of reality given that all the people on this planet were idiot civilians who had no idea just how much danger they were in. There was no way that they would have taken xyr warning seriously, if they even got it.

"What I wouldn't give for interstellar comms right now." Payton sighed.

"My people still have them," Shani said, fidgeting until Narcisse wrapped her arms around Shani's neck. "I have no doubt that the

Drath High Council is throwing a snit fit. None of us like the Women of the Sea."

"Just the Drath or all the other races?" Narcisse asked.

"Oh, all of us," Shani huffed and snapped at the air like she wanted to bite someone. "They're only about half a million years younger than the Drath and absolutely convinced that they're our equals. Most of the other races think that they're superior to every other race, of course. It's a common trait, but the Women of the Sea take it to extremes."

"Hmm," Narcisse hummed, eyes distant. She shook her head, a frown blooming abruptly. "They certainly aren't polite about their opinions."

"Stop listening to them," Payton snapped at her.

Xe glowered when Narcisse just frowned up at xem. How hard was it to keep from blowing up your own brain? Seriously, aneurism wasn't something to risk. Even Gensyn nanites had trouble with aneurisms in the brain stem and brain core.

Narcisse sighed. "Fine. It's hard to ignore them. Especially when they're right underneath the yacht."

Payton promptly grabbed for his grenades while Tracey jerked at the wheel of the boat.

"No, no, not like they're tracking us," Narcisse huffed, waving for Tracey and Payton to both stop. "It's just that they're way down near the sea floor and we happen to be passing overtop of them. I don't think they even realize that we're here. We're like ants to them or something."

"Definitely like ants," Shani agreed. Her tail drooped, as did her ears. "I don't think that any of the races would take humanity seriously. Your technology is, ah, primitive."

"Mmm," Narcisse agreed while Payton glowered at the polite little insult. "But we still cover a huge territory and we've integrated fully into each solar system we find as the dominant predator. Can any of the other species say that?"

Shani sneeze-laughed, tail going into tight enough loops that Payton was surprised she didn't give herself a cramp. "No, actually. Not even we can say that. None of us do that. Humans are the only intelligent species we've found, space-faring or not, that expanded out of their home solar system without FTL drives. You're also the only one that adapts to all environments. It's confusing. Fascinating, but confusing."

"Well, then," Narcisse said brightly even though she still had that wrinkle between her eyebrows and her eyes were still slightly unfocused, "obviously we're people to be worried about. Unpredictable and violent and uncontrollable."

"We are that," Payton agreed as Shani wheezed with laughter and Tracey grinned at the horizon that she hadn't stopped scanning for threats.

Of course, that didn't mean that they were going to survive this encounter. You know, personally. Just because the human species as a whole were predators that adapted to every environment they could find didn't mean that particular individuals, Payton and Narcisse and Tracey, would survive what was coming their way.

Payton checked xyr ammo again, eyes on the horizon as xe scanned for threats.

Maybe not, but Payton was going to do xyr damnedest to see all four of them made it through, no matter what the sea aliens, the ground-pounders or the Drath threw xyr way.

NINETEEN
ACROSS CHOPPY WATERS

HALF AN HOUR of rest was a lovely thing. Just enough to take the edge off and let Shani's hackles slowly go down. Narcisse sat cuddled against her side, rubbing her back gently and letting her nails scratch that spot between Shani's shoulder blades that made her ears go floppy and her eyes drift mostly shut.

They'd claimed a spot on the floor near the door. Narcisse had her chemical grenades carefully set on the floor, set just far enough apart that the vibration of the engine or movement of the ocean waves under the yacht didn't make them knock together. It would be a terrible shame if one of them went off. Payton might survive it. Narcisse and Tracey definitely wouldn't.

Who knew about Shani?

What mattered was that Payton had put together two oversized slingshot things that would let them loft the grenades through the air at attacking ships. Xe prowled around the deck, for all the world on patrol even though there wasn't anything incoming that they could see.

"How long until we hit the mainland?" Narcisse asked Tracey.

"Three hours," Tracey replied, checking the scanners. "If we make it."

The yacht had scanners both for overhead and under the surface of the water. The former owner of the yacht must have enjoyed deep sea fishing. Narcisse couldn't see either set of scanners from her spot on the floor, but Tracey's scent was nervous, determined, and alert, not pissed off that the next round of attacks were there.

There would be another round of attacks. That was inevitable, really. The Women of the Sea still muttered away in the back of Narcisse's head, complaining about being pulled back, complaining about children who didn't understand the level of threat they, individually, were facing, complaining about vermin ruining their excellent plan for ensuring that they would control the galaxy.

The opening movements of a war; that's what this was. Narcisse wasn't sure why it had broken out here, why now, but she recognized it nonetheless. Mother's fascination with Old Earth's ancient wars made the pattern so very clear.

World War II started in much the same way with an apparently insignificant assassination of a minor official setting the brewing tensions between the nations of the world afire. Shani's scent went bitter with worry and guilt.

"Oh, hush," Narcisse murmured while hugging Shani. "None of this is your fault, dear. I'd bet that this has been brewing for dozens of years, maybe hundreds. It's not you at all. This just happens to be the point where things blew up."

"I know," Shani groaned. She flopped on the floor, hiding her snout under her stubby little paw-hands. "I know, but I still feel so bad about dragging the two of you into this."

"Drag nothing," Tracey drawled. "Narcisse leaped straight into it feet first, claws out, the moment she met you. There's no dragging going on. And yeah, I think Narcisse is right. We're just the flashpoint for a long-simmering Cold War to go hot. I mean, seriously, how long have you and the other space-faring species been at each other's throats?"

"...Oh, easily three million years," Shani said, one ear rotating like a windmill. Or like Narcisse would've rotated one hand when she wanted to convey that sense of thinking about something for a long time. "The Women of the Sea keep kicking things up a notch every chance they get even though they're one of the youngest of the space-faring species. They've only been colonizing new worlds for about two hundred and fifty thousand years. They take their time on the ecological transformations of their worlds, so they spread slowly."

"This is one of their colony worlds, then," Narcisse said thoughtfully. "Hm. I'm sure they'll claim that they had every right to do what they did when Drath arrived on "their" world."

"Pretty much," Shani agreed. She sighed gustily, ears going back as she snarled. "But I checked before we debarked. They never filed a claim on this solar system. There's a whole process for making sure that we don't intrude on each other's territory. There's no paperwork anywhere showing that they'd begun work on this world or that they wanted to expand in this direction."

A slowly worsening Cold War sounded about right, then. Narcisse hummed as she petted Shani. She certainly had no idea how the galactic politics worked. Humanity as a whole had been told quite firmly that they were too young and too technologically undeveloped to be admitted as a proper space-faring species.

Which implied there were other intelligent species out there that weren't spacefaring. Possibly just as advanced or more advanced than the Drath. Fascinating thought. Narcisse was kind of glad that she hadn't encountered any. Who knew what might happen?

One of the Women of the Sea chime-crooned something encouraging.

"Tracey, check for threats," Narcisse ordered.

"Oh, great," Tracey complained while checking every scanner the yacht had. "What now?"

"Not sure."

Shani tensed under Narcisse's hands as the seconds ticked on. Outside, Payton suddenly stiffened, eyes locked on the horizon. At the same moment, Tracey started cursing. As Shani scrambled to her feet, Narcisse sighed and stood as well.

There were boats on the horizon. And flyers, three of them.

"Lovely." Narcisse groaned. "All right, warn them off on the grounds of Drath High Command being ready to inflict orbital bombardment on anyone stopping us from getting to the mainland."

"Comms are jammed," Tracey replied. She glowered at the boats and flyers coming at them. "I'm getting really sick of jammed comms."

"Incoming!" Payton snapped. "Narcisse, get ready with your grenades. I can take the flyers out, but the grenades will probably be needed soon."

The oncoming boats, plural, roared straight at them, bouncing across the surface of the ocean like skipped rocks. Overhead, two of the flyers went into a strafing run that led to Payton blowing them out of the sky. The third one swooped up high into the sky and then got shot in the ass. It spiraled down into the ocean, billowing smoke.

The third flyer exploded just before it hit the surface of the water.

Narcisse loaded one of her gas grenades into the makeshift slingshot that Payton had created. There boats coming at them were fast, yes, but what mattered was that they had force fields over them. Maybe not strong enough to block every single weapon that Payton had stolen, but more than enough to make Payton's shots worryingly ineffective.

"Damn them!" Payton shouted when xyr first shot at one of the boats splattered out on the force field.

"Let's see what range I've got here," Narcisse said as she did a quick calculation in her head, considering the relative velocities of the boats versus the yacht, and then lobbed the first grenade high in the air.

Narcisse ducked down and covered her head as soon as the grenade left her slingshot.

Six seconds later, the grenade exploded in a shattering crack that sprayed a flaming cloud of toxic gas and burning chemicals over about twenty square meters of the ocean. When Narcisse peeked, the chemicals kept right on burning as they sank into the ocean. She smiled and grabbed another one.

This time she sent it on a straight, flat trajectory right at the closest attack boat.

The force field that worked so very well for plasma blasters did not much at all for a chunk of glass filled with toxic chemicals. Instead of blocking it, the force field broke the glass, freed the chemicals to mix, and one second later the fireball and cloud of toxic gas enveloped the attack boat.

Narcisse pressed her lips together so that she wouldn't scream. Or shout triumphantly. That... was exactly the sort of death she wanted to avoid every day at work. Seeing it and knowing how the attackers' flesh melted, their lungs boiled before they died, was not... good.

"Yes!" Payton shouted at the same time Tracey cheered. "Fuck yes!"

The two remaining attack boats swerved off so abruptly that Narcisse almost missed the vividly purple cursing of the Woman of the Sea underneath them. Narcisse huffed and lobbed a grenade over the side of the boat. This time it took about ten seconds for the chemicals to combine, much too variable to be an effective and safe weapon.

Behind them, the surface of the ocean bloomed up in a geyser of water mixed with flames that looked like the embodiment of Hell. In the back of Narcisse's mind, the Woman of the Sea gasped and jetted away, swimming deeper and deeper to escape the burning chemicals drifting down through the water column at her.

"What was that for?" Tracey asked.

"Woman of the Sea underneath us, too close," Narcisse explained. "Two attack boats left."

"On one," Payton called as xe loaded in a gas grenade as if it was made of spun sugar and filled with the strongest acid.

Xe was even better at trajectories than Narcisse because Payton's shot went a little high and to the left of one attack boat, and then managed, somehow, to land exactly where the second boat was just as it passed.

That explosion hit hard enough to make the remaining attack boat skip and stutter and then flip over as its hydroplane collapsed in the suddenly ruffled water's surface. Payton cheered; one fist thrust up into the air in victory.

But the roiled water made the yacht shudder and bounce. Narcisse frowned, scanning the waters. The area around the yacht was bubbling. No water around them out about ten meters was bubbling.

"Attack under the water!" Narcisse shouted to Payton. "Throw more grenades into the water, quick!"

Narcisse only had one of her chemical grenades left. She threw it hard and then scrambled for one of Payton's proper grenades. That got tossed just as the first explosion went off. On the other side of the yacht, Payton cursed as xe threw one of Narcisse's grenades, then two real grenades, then the final of Narcisse's grenades.

The explosion this time was deafening. Water and flaming chemicals blasted up into the air all around them. Narcisse rolled away from the raining, scrambling to her feet to get inside. Payton did the same on the far side of the yacht.

"Something's dragging at us," Tracey snarled as she pushed the yacht engines as hard as she could.

"They changed the water around us," Narcisse reported. "It's bubbling. Lower tensile strength, less propulsion."

"...They can do that?" Tracey asked, horrified, as she stared at Shani.

"Yes." Shani shuddered; tail tucked beneath her again. "And so much more. I don't know why they haven't sunk the--"

White.

The sound so loud that it was a physical impact instead of a noise.

Narcisse found herself lying on the floor, curled under the yacht control panel. Her nose bled. So did her eyes and ears. Tracey lay next to Narcisse, shaking.

Payton loomed over the two of them, a thin stream of blood rapidly drying under xyr nose. Xe steered the yacht, lips moving in curses that Narcisse could smell but could not hear. Yet.

Orbital strike.

Narcisse struggled to her hands and knees. She crawled over to Shani who lay shaking and curled into a ball with her tail wrapped all the way around her body. Fetal position. That had to be the Drath version of fetal position.

As Narcisse hugged Shani, Tracey shook her head and scrambled to her feet. She looked out the rear windows and then screamed something that made no sense to Narcisse.

Except that it did.

Orbital strike. Ocean.

Tsunami.

There was a tsunami of water coming at them. There had to be. The fear and confusion in Tracey's scent didn't match that, though.

Narcisse kissed Shani's neck and struggled to her feet.

No, there was no tsunami. The water behind the yacht was smooth as glass. Yes, there was another mushroom cloud rising from the ocean's surface, but the Women of the Sea had apparently decided not to allow the impact to disturb their oceans.

They had locked the water's chemical bonds into a rapidly expanding sheet of ice that looked as though it was growing downwards even faster than it was chasing the yacht. Narcisse sucked in a breath and let it out slowly.

Her whole body shook.

This was not something that Narcisse could fight. It wasn't something that any of them could fight. A power like that? Humans were actually ants compared to that.

Her ears popped as Narcisse's nanites repaired the damage to her eardrums and inner ears from the orbital strike.

"What the hell?" Tracey chanted as she took the wheel from Payton. "What the hell? What the hell?"

"We are so fucking dead," Payton complained in bitter counterpoint to Tracey's chant.

Narcisse kept watching the Women of the Sea work. To her surprise, Shani shuddered, shook herself and then stood on legs that trembled. At least until she leaned into Narcisse's side.

"How much power could they have here?" Narcisse asked Shani.

The ice's progress wasn't keeping pace with the yacht.

The bubbling of the water around the yacht had stopped while Narcisse and Tracey were down.

Their power couldn't be infinite.

"Not enough to fight directly," Shani replied. "But more than enough to kill us."

Narcisse hummed as she caressed Shani's ears, her muscular neck and shoulders. "Really? I don't know if that's true, actually. The ice isn't keeping pace."

Both Payton and Tracey stopped cursing. They looked over their shoulders. Tracey straightened. Grinned. And then pushed the yacht back to full speed.

"Thank fuck for that," Payton said. "We have an hour to the mainland and then we have to get Shani back to her people."

"Good," Narcisse said, watching the ice while doing calculations in her head. "It will be close, I think, but we might just make it in time."

Orbital strike versus the power available to keep the impact from disturbing the oceans. Narcisse wasn't sure which would win, Women of the Sea or the Drath. But if they could get off the ocean fast enough, it wouldn't be their battle to fight anymore.

Leave the battles of giants to the giants. Narcisse only cared about getting Shani safe. Everything else could wait.

TWENTY
GUARD AGAINST DEATH ITSELF

THE MOMENT THAT THE LONG, dark smudge of the mainland appeared on the horizon was perhaps the very best moment of Payton's entire fucking life. Xe blew out a breath, glowered at the ocean around the stupid boat, and went back to patrolling the deck in determined counter-clockwise circles.

Not a hell of a lot else xe could do. The grenades Narcisse had made were long-gone. Most of Payton's regular grenades were gone, too. Virtually every single weapon xe had besides the remaining handful of grenades were useless against the sea aliens.

Fucking water. Xe never had liked large bodies of water. Too dangerous and really only good for breeding fish to eat while filtering out excessive radiation. Water like this, just lying around doing nothing good, was a horror. Except, sadly, it looked like the sea aliens were making great strides in using the ocean in ways that Payton wouldn't have dreamed even in his worst nightmares.

The ice forming across the ocean for no damned reason at all, wasn't too far behind them.

It grew in surges, like the sea water suddenly crystallized in a chunk, instead of slowly growing the way ice should form. Payton paused at the back of the boat, staring at the shimmering white mass of ice lying across the tropics of this hell-planet.

Then xe swallowed down the terror clawing a scream up xyr throat and scanned the skies and seas for more human threats. All three of them agreed that there would be more human threats. How could there not be?

The sea aliens were absolutely going to try something. Narcisse couldn't tell what, not when Shani nudged and made sad puppy eyes at her every single time Narcisse so much as looked thoughtful.

Payton made another seventy-one circuits of the deck as Tracey flung their stolen boat right at the mainland. As the shore grew and grew, forming houses built into the hillsides and buzzing flyers going about their normal business as if the Drath hadn't hammered their world with two orbital strikes already, Payton slipped into the cockpit.

"What's the plan?" Payton asked.

"Ram the yacht into whatever dry land we can find," Tracey announced, "and then run for the hills."

"Preferably somewhere on the edge of town instead of right in the middle," Narcisse observed with a quiet, thoughtful hum.

"Why?" Tracey asked. Her fingers tightened on the wheel until her claws came out, staining it with venom.

"Because we know that the Women of the Sea are controlling people," Narcisse said. "The police will be clustered in the center of town. If we land there, there's less of a chance that we can get someone unaffected. We need outer edges so that we can get away from shore and then find some sort of comms or transportation."

"My team should be not too far outside of the capital," Shani said, dancing in place nervously. Her ears were right back against her skull and her eyes way too wide. Even her nostrils kept flaring as if she was trying to smell everything that might be a threat.

Actually, that's probably exactly what she was doing. Right. Okay.

"Is that the capital?" Payton asked because xe hadn't paid attention to where they landed. What did xe care about local politics? This was an easy escort job with no threats at all.

Yeah, never making that mistake again.

"Yep," Tracey confirmed grimly. "Okay, get ready. I see boats incoming and flyers heading our way. We can't assume they're enemies, but the comms are still out so we can't confirm either way."

"Warning shots across their noses it is," Payton said as xe headed back out onto the deck.

Payton lifted xyr blaster rifle to xyr shoulder, watching as the flyers moved into a circling pattern instead of coming for a strafing run. None of them seemed to have weapons hot, but Payton didn't let xyr guard down. The boats swooped in as if they were going to come alongside.

"No, you don't," Payton said.

Xe fired a warning shot at the lead boat, hitting the ocean near enough to it that water sprayed over the occupants. One of them visibly threw up their arms to cover xyr head. Payton could see the wide eyes and shock on their faces.

Xe kept the rifle at the ready.

The escort boats moved into a wide bracket around them. That was... more acceptable. Mostly. Payton didn't like an escort at all, but if they were going to keep their distance and keep weapons holstered, xe would put up with it.

"They seem okay," Narcisse observed from the doorway. "I don't hear any chatter from the Women of the Sea."

"Don't fucking care," Payton replied. "No one gets close. We don't let up the guard until we get Shani back to her people."

"Agreed," Narcisse said. "I'll take the other side. Be careful. Just because I can't hear them, doesn't mean they're not there."

"Exactly what I'm worried about." Payton sighed and jerked xyr chin for Narcisse to take up her post on the far side of the cockpit.

Their trick of running the boat up onto the shore wasn't going to work with this huge thing, no matter what Tracey wanted to believe. It was too big, too much of a deep belly. They'd get stuck before the water ran out and then have to jump into the water.

Payton was not letting Shani jump into the water, even if she would.

That meant that they needed docks, wharfs or something. Payton scanned the shoreline, picking out the low smudges of docks amid the profusion of frilly fern trees and fern shrubs. Thank fuck, the mainland had a lot less spikey palm trees and a lot more soft-edged ferns. Payton healed fast enough that the palms hadn't done xem any damage, but getting shredded was never fun.

Tracey steered the boat away from the center of town with its big, heavy wharf and profusion of docks. The instant they diverged from the expected, and idiotic, path, the circling boats and flyers closed in as if to force them back on path.

Narcisse fired a warning shot just before Payton got xyr rifle on xyr shoulder.

The flyers pulled way back. The boats wavered, skittering away and then back and then settling a few hundred meters further away than they had been. Payton nodded. Just what they should do.

Which meant everything was perfect. Tracey shouted triumphantly as she found the perfect dock for them to rush up on. The boats and flyers were well out of range so that they could all run right off the boat and onto dry land. It was all going the way Payton wanted.

"When are they going to act?" Payton called to Narcisse. "You know it's going too smoothly!"

"Agreed!" Tracey's snarl was visible through the windows.

Narcisse stood calm and distant-eyed on the far side of the boat. She cocked her head to the side as if listening to the sea aliens again. Even Shani reaching her tail-hand out to poke Narcisse in the side didn't make her stop.

"Oh, that's not good," Narcisse said. "Fog! Deadly fog. Go straight through it, Tracey. Crash into shore if you have to. We need to be through the fog as fast as possible."

"What fog?" Payton asked at the same time as Tracey.

Xe turned towards the shore which rushed at them full speed even though the boat on Payton's side waved urgently for them to slow down.

Fog billowed up off the water, so thick that it looked like a wall. There was a smell of salt to it that Payton realized xe knew. They'd gone through this fog before, on their way out to the islands. Shani had gotten sick as soon as they landed but the smell of salt and the dampness of the fog had lingered long after they passed through the fog bank.

Payton flung xemself inside, grabbing Narcisse and hauling her in, too. Then xe dashed down the stairwell, scrambling for beach towels. Xe went back up the stairs three at a time. Shani yipped and nearly bit Payton as xe flung towels around her body, but Narcisse gasped and nodded urgently.

"Electrical tape," Tracey said, tossing a roll over her shoulder. "Hurry!"

The swaddling of blankets was nowhere near enough to cover all of Shani's body. She was long and lean with so much leg and tail that there was no chance that they could cover her up entirely. Payton did xyr best with Narcisse's help. At least they got her head, neck and body covered.

Legs and tail would just have to be uncovered because Tracey shouted a wordless warning just before the boat hull screeched and boomed.

Impact.

Payton let the impact carry xem forward. Xe kept xyr arms around Shani, not surprised that Narcisse did the same thing. What surprised xem was that Tracey took a running leap and went straight through the forward windshield, spraying glass all across the front of the boat.

Shani scrambled to her feet and leaped straight through the opening Tracey had made. She was up the dock and heading for the hills long before Tracey disappeared into the fog. Payton grabbed for Narcisse's arm. She grabbed back, hauling Payton along with her into the sticky damp fog that couldn't possibly be natural.

Wasn't the easiest thing Payton had ever done, running along the deck of a crashing boat, but xe did it. The dock bucked like it'd been hit by an asteroid strike, nearly tossing both Payton and Narcisse into the water. Between Payton grabbing at one of the log-support things and Narcisse using her claws a few steps later to keep them from tumbling into the water, the two of them made it to shore.

Narcisse scrubbed at her nose, sniffed the air, and then set off running towards the right.

The fog was so thick that Payton kept all xyr attention on staying with her. Narcisse could find Shani and Tracey. Payton couldn't. He didn't have their noses or tracking ability.

Fuck, it was odd not to be the most terrifying thing in the area.

They ran full-on up a street that curved to the left, heading uphill. The fog was so thick that Payton couldn't see more than the next step xe took. It was like running in a nightmare, as if xe wasn't actually running, just pumping xyr arms and legs while hovering in space.

Narcisse led them up a flight of steep stone stairs cut into the hillside, off to the left, then right up another set of stairs. Then there was a winding road that switch-backed up a hillside so steep that Payton couldn't have climbed it without getting on xyr hands and feet.

They went leaping from curb to retaining wall to curb, Narcisse hauling Payton up each time xe missed a landing or struggled to keep up. At the top, Narcisse scrubbed at her nose and then nodded firmly before leading Payton through a courtyard surrounded by cheerful stone houses painted in bright colors that xe could barely see through the damned fog.

They careened out onto another street, going ever upwards. In the distance Payton heard sirens screaming. There were alarms starting to go off behind them, a growing cacophony of them that set the hair on the back of Payton's neck stand up with fear.

Something was happening.

"I know!" Narcisse snapped at Payton. "Keep up!"

"Doing… my… best!" Payton panted.

Xyr best wasn't good enough.

Narcisse gasped, suddenly back-pedaling as her eyes went wide. Caught off guard, Payton smacked into her and knocked them both down. All around them, alarms started going off in the quiet stone houses.

Payton dragged Narcisse back to her feet as xe grabbed for a weapon even though xe had no idea what they were up against now. Traitors? Mind-controlled guards? Those damned sea aliens riding up in balls of water like the little plastic balls Payton's tiniest cousins gave to their hamsters?

"Run!" Tracey shouted as she appeared out of the fog with Shani loping, limping, at her side.

Before Payton could turn, before xe could run or shoot into the fog, something hit xem in the chest hard enough to break most of xyr ribs.

Blood sprayed until xyr heart slowed down and all of Payton's blood vessels constricted to keep xyr blood inside xyr body.

As xe toppled, xe saw Tracey gasp and fall to the ground with a set of tranquilizer darts traced up her right thigh and back. Narcisse dove over Shani, taking two tranquilizers. Shani shuddered and collapsed.

Just like she had when they reached the island.

The sea aliens had Shani again.

And their allies, their puppets, had all four of them.

TWENTY-ONE
THE ENEMY WITHIN

THERE WAS A TRICK TO TRANQUILIZERS.

Narcisse hadn't ever had the chance to teach Tracey about them, but it was fairly simple. As she toppled on top of Shani, Narcisse jammed her claws into her thigh where the tranquilizers had impacted.

The burn of her venom tore through Narcisse's flesh, sending her body's immune system and circulatory system into a frenzy to drive the venom out. It didn't stop Narcisse from graying out, but the world disappeared down a long, grey, echoing tunnel instead of falling into complete blackness.

The hands that grabbed Narcisse weren't gentle. Even with the distance the tranquilizers gave her, she could tell that her captors were annoyed. She got tossed into a transport of some sort. Tracey was tossed next to Narcisse, out to the world. By her scent's density, she'd be out for hours. Shani was dropped at Narcisse's feet.

"The body?" one of the captors asked.

"Oh, that's a Gensyn," another captor said. "Xe're not dead, just passed out. Hell, we could probably chop off a limb and it still wouldn't kill xem. Might even reattach if we put the severed limb next to the open wound. Toss xem in the back with those women and the Drath. We're on a time line, here."

There wasn't enough blood scent as Payton dropped next to Tracey. Odd. Narcisse had seen the needles tear through Payton's chest, tear out xyr guts and knock xem over onto xyr back. Xyr eyes had stared up at the foggy sky as unseeingly as any dead animal that Narcisse had ever killed.

But xe didn't smell dead at all. Actually, Payton's scent was much more alive and shifting than Tracey's. Their captors must be right that Payton wasn't down at all. Xe were going to wake up much sooner than Tracey.

Maybe soon enough?

"Got them," the first captor called. "Go!"

The transport jerked into motion. Not soon enough, damn it all.

"What the hell is with these guys, anyway?" the first captor asked. Their boot nudged Narcisse's thigh. "There's warnings all over the net about them."

"I don't know, and I don't care," the second captor replied far too grimly. "Command wants them contained. They're getting contained. That's all that matters."

"Yeah, but, what about that whole orbital strike thing?"

First Captor was apparently the young and stubborn sort. Narcisse almost wanted to bless him for keeping on with the questions, but not really because she was sure that he was watching all four of them for any signs of waking up. Her body was starting to shake as she fought off the venom and the tranquilizers. If he saw that, he'd hit her with more of them and then they would be doomed.

"That wasn't an orbital strike," Second Captor said so grumpily that Narcisse suspected that it was the dozenth or so time they'd had the conversation. "They were just comets, that's all. For fuck's sake, it happens."

"Not without notice from orbital control," First Captor complained under his breath.

Good on him. He might be too willing to follow orders he didn't understand, but he at least questioned them.

Narcisse focused on keeping her body as still as she could. Her hands shook, but the transport vibrated enough that it hopefully didn't show too badly. After a few moments of silence, First Captor moved to poking Tracey in the side, then Shani who whimpered and kicked feebly.

There was no response from Payton.

Yet.

That whimper bothered Shani, though. Shani smelled much the same as she had when they first met, sick and weak and exhausted. The fog must have had the effect that Payton feared. Her fur must be infested with whatever those things were again. And this time it would be much harder to remove them because first, she had so much less fur, and second, they didn't have a cave that they could contain the things in.

Who knew how much they would grow if given free rein?

Getting it off Shani was important. Hitting Tracey with some venom, preferably her own, was a priority. Keeping their captors from realizing that Narcisse was only about two minutes away from fully functional was the most important thing.

The transport was one of the wheeled variety, not a flyer, so they couldn't go too far. The mainland had several nice-sized settlements that were connected by rail. There were no roads that went between the cities. Why bother when you could fly so much faster?

So there was only so far their captors could take them.

Narcisse didn't work her fingers as they tingled back to life. She didn't wiggle her toes even though the pins and needles were horribly annoying. Showing that she was awake wasn't a good idea.

"Where are we going?" First Captor asked. He sounded entirely too close, like he was looming right over Narcisse.

She twitched despite her best efforts to pay dead.

"Why?"

"I don't know how long they're gonna stay out," First Captor replied. "I mean, the Gensyn has started twitching despite the hole blown through xyr chest. Which, you know, is closing up fast. And the busty girl's kind of twitching, too. You know, sleepy twitches? Not like, full-on wake up but not really asleep."

"Oh, shit," Second Captor whined. "We're ten minutes out! Hit them both with more tranquilizers!"

Narcisse hurled herself upwards, grabbing for First Captor before she even got her eyes open. The tranquilizers had done a number on her eyes. Everything was blurry, too blurry to make anything out.

Didn't matter.

Her nose filled with the stench of terror from First Captor as Narcisse latched her claws around his throat and pulled. Blood sprayed everywhere, coating Narcisse. The spray stopped a moment later, before First Captor's body hit the floor. Her venom had already stopped his heart.

Narcisse whirled and jumped over Shani, Tracey and Payton to wrap her claws around Second Captor's neck.

"You will not take us there," Narcisse hissed in his ear.

"Get the fuck off me!" Second Captor screamed as he jerked the wheel of the transport.

"Careful," Narcisse said, displaying her claws in front of his face. "I'm venomous, darling. Your friend is already dead."

"Oh, shit. Oh, shit. Oh, shit," Second Captor whimpered.

He very carefully righted the transport, scent full of determination to take them where they were "supposed" to go.

"Darling, I will kill you and toss your body in the back with your friend if you do that," Shani said. "I can smell what you're thinking."

"What the fuck are you?" Second Captor cried.

"A predator," Narcisse said. "Take us to the Drath. Now!"

"They're not even on planet anymore!" Second Captor exclaimed.

"I don't believe you," Narcisse sang in his ear. "Take us to their base now or I tear your throat out, darling."

She wanted to check on Shani. She wanted to see if she could do something to help Payton heal faster. She really wanted to treat Tracey so that she would wake up faster.

Narcisse did none of that.

She kept her claws around Second Captor's throat, kept reminding him that he would die if he didn't follow orders, and kept blinking her eyes as she waited for the tranquilizers to abate enough that she could see.

They moved out of the city, away from the lovely little stone houses with their brightly painted walls. The farms outside of the city trundled past. Narcisse wasn't sure that this was where the Drath were staying.

She did know that Second Captor had turned north instead of continuing east. He certainly smelled as though he was doing as Narcisse wanted.

"...Fuck...ing... hell."

Narcisse grinned over her shoulder. "About time you started waking up. Where were the Drath staying?"

"Camp... north of... the capital," Payton wheezed.

Xe looked about half healed. Xyr chest had closed up again, broken ribs knitting back together. The wound in xyr stomach gleamed wetly, but xe wasn't bleeding. As Narcisse watched, the stomach wound gradually grew back together.

"Good," Narcisse said. "Check Shani when you can. And if you can, later when you can move, stab Tracey with her own claws. It'll help her metabolize the tranquilizers."

"You... two are... terrifying," Payton complained.

"Says the person who had xyr heart blown up," Narcisse huffed.

Second Captor giggled wetly at the teasing. His hands shook on the wheel, but he managed to steer them straight up the road.

Which was empty of other traffic.

Narcisse sighed and petting Second Captor's cheek with her claws. "They know where we're going, don't they, darling?"

"Please don't kill me!" Second Captor cried, actually cried with tears rolling down his cheeks.

"Then answer my question," Narcisse replied.

"Of fucking course they do!" Second Captor complained. "There's trackers on the transport and everyone on the planet knows about your rampage. They had to have cleared the roads the instant we went this direction. There's alarms all over the place telling people to stay indoors so that you don't kill them."

"Mmm, good," Narcisse said. "Less collateral damage. Pick up the pace."

"What?" Second Captor nearly twisted around to stare at Narcisse. Only her claws tightening around his throat made him stop.

"You won't have traffic to worry about," Narcisse said. "Pick up the pace."

He whined but he did it. They went from a steady trundle to a careening rush up the road. It didn't take long before they reached the end of the paved section. Gravel made for a much rougher ride.

Narcisse had to switch her grip on Second Captor so that she didn't accidentally tear his throat out. If she was going to do it, she wanted it to be on purpose. At this point, Narcisse was fairly certain that it would happen.

Second Captor smelled too frustrated to keep himself alive. Fear was obviously not a good enough motivator for him.

About the time they went from gravel to raw earth wheel tracks through fern and reed grass, Payton managed to roll over. Narcisse talked him through stabbing Tracey with her own claws, though both Second Captor and Payton looked at her like she was insane.

"Just do it," Narcisse said. "We need Tracey up and running as soon as possible."

"Fine," Payton grumbled.

The dose of venom was almost certainly not enough, but it was better than nothing. Payton collapsed back to the floor of the van next to Tracey who started shivering.

Shani didn't move at all.

As flyers started moving in from the east and west, Second Captor slowed the transport to a slow roll. He stopped it in the middle of a wide open field with fern trees around the perimeter and low red flowers carpeting the ground. He shut off the transport and then glowered at Narcisse.

"This is it," Second Captor said belligerently even with Narcisse's claws prickling against his thigh. "I told you. They're gone. No base, no tents, no nothing."

"You're an idiot," Narcisse huffed. "Payton, was their base underground?"

"Of fucking course it was underground," Payton grumbled as xe struggled to sit up. Xe managed to get up on one elbow before sliding back down with a moan. "They live in burrows. They wouldn't put anything on the surface."

Narcisse turned back to Second Captor who'd gone bone-white. His eyes went wide enough that they were white all the way around. Then he flung himself towards the cabin door, trying to escape Narcisse and her claws.

Waste of time on his part. A single claw though the fabric of his pants and he died slumping out of the cabin door. Narcisse pushed him out and then sniffed the air.

Someday, long after this was over, Narcisse was going to have a long cry. Then she was going to need a massive amount of therapy.

Not now.

Not until Shani and Tracey and Payton were safe.

There was something here. No doubt about that. She could smell the cinnamon-musk scent of Drath, different ones from Shani. They didn't smell especially recent, but that could just be because they weren't on the surface. The scents were complex enough that Narcisse rubbed her nose against the need to sneeze.

"Where's the door?" Narcisse asked Payton as she restarted the transport. "I'll get us as close as possible."

"Big rock," Payton said, panting. Xyr eyes were shut, and sweat had beaded up all over xyr forehead. "Flat, set into the ground. Dead-center of the clearing. Should be right next to it. If it's open."

"Big rock it is," Narcisse said, heading for the center of the clearing.

Even if none of the other Drath were in their base, there should be medical supplies. Drath comms. Something that would let Narcisse save Shani. Just a bit more and Shani would be safe.

Hopefully.

TWENTY-TWO
BROKEN TRUST AND HONOR

THE DOOR into the Drath base was closed, because of course it was. Payton cursed under xyr panting breath. Xyr whole body ached, especially xyr guts. Getting intestines blown out was so awful. Xe hated that. Almost as bad as getting limbs lopped off and having to suffer through the nerves reattaching once the limb was put back in place.

Every wheezing, bubbling breath pulled xyr fragmented ribs. Every movement made xyr legs tremble, but Payton still did xyr best to keep up with Narcisse. Didn't work.

She was a woman on a mission, just as she had been since the moment they met.

Payton had met Gensyn generals who were less focused, less determined and a hell of a lot less dangerous than fragile, sweet, kind, deadly Narcisse. Xe didn't see what happened to the people who caught them. Didn't need to. The blood sprays in the back of the transport and across the inside of the cab door told the story for her.

Narcisse frowned as she sniffed around the big flat rock. She'd already gone over the spot where the door had been. It should've been obvious where it was. Big ass hole in the ground with a nice rough-textured ramp that felt like raw dirt under your boots but wasn't actually was not something that just disappeared.

Except that it had.

The spot where the door had been looked like the reed-grass and those weird liver-shaped red flowers had never once been disturbed in millions of years. Payton leaned against the front bumper of the transport; one arm wrapped around xyr aching ribs. Gently. Carefully. The bones were still so weakly fused that xe could probably crush xyr own ribcage with no effort.

"There is something here," Narcisse said, nose in the dirt as she crouched on hands and knees. "I can smell it. Can't figure out how to open it, but it's here."

"You're not Drath," Payton observed. "There's no way you could open it. I didn't spend much time in their base, but I do know that they weren't eager to give humans of any race access to their tech."

"Oh, totally agreed," Narcisse said as she slowly ran her fingertips over the edge of the big flat rock. "Humans are horrible scavengers. We would do something stupid with their tech. That's just how we are."

Despite that, Narcisse still hunted all over the stone and surrounding territory. Payton slowly eased xyr way down to sit on the bumper of the transport. It hurt to brace xemself but xe didn't think xe could get back up from the ground without help. A lot of help.

"All right," Narcisse said finally about five minutes later. "I think I've figured it out, but I need Shani."

"She's not moving," Payton said as xe slowly, painfully, hauled xemself back to xyr feet.

"I know," Narcisse said.

She bit her lip before marching right past Payton into the transport. By the time xe got to the big door on the side of the thing, Narcisse was crouched over Shani, whispering encouragement to her.

Tracey lay, out to the world, twitching next to the blankets that had been wrapped around Shani. None of them showed any signs of the creepy nanite attacker things that'd been in Shani's fur back on the island. Payton had no doubt they were there whether xe could see them or not.

All xe had to do was look at Shani to see that she was suffering the same shit all over again, damn it all.

"Shani, you don't open the fucking door and we can't purge whatever those sea aliens did to you," Payton announced loud enough to make both Shani and Narcisse jerk in surprise. "You got the only paws that'll open it."

"They'll come," Shani said, hoarse as if she'd gargled glass. Sounded more like a growl than her normal musical voice.

"Of course they will," Payton said. Xe met Narcisse's furious glower squarely. "They're probably on the way. You gotta let your people know what happened to you. You gotta get purged of those nanite things. And the only way that's gonna happen is inside the base. So slap your tail against the ground and shove your way back to your feet. Firing a blaster will probably knock me flat again, but I've got your back. They won't get you without going through me first."

Shani stared at Payton for a long moment. Too long. Her ears rotated from alert and pointing at him to flat against her skull. Her tail-hand shook, and her paws kept flexing so that her stubby claws scraped against the floor of the transport.

Then she nodded and did just as Payton had said.

It took her tail, all four paws, and Narcisse's assistance to get Shani to the doorway. Narcisse had to hold Shani up as she worked the lock. Payton watched for a moment before shaking his head.

Xe didn't need to know how the door worked. Let Narcisse handle that. Payton scanned the skies and turned the comms in the transport up enough that xe could hear it while standing outside of the door.

They were scratchy but quiet, definitely working though no one said a thing. Xe wasn't surprised by comm silence. Payton would've had everyone shut up and get off the comms right about the time the first attack happened outside the restaurant. By the time they were on the boat between islands, Payton would've shot anyone who broke comm silence in the head.

Apparently, the locals weren't as big on proper information control because they'd been idiots for ages about comms. And everything else, too.

"Got it!" Narcisse exclaimed.

"You need... to stay in the doorway," Shani told Payton. "The security system will lock up again if there's not someone there."

"...Right."

Payton hobbled over and stood in the doorway as Narcisse helped, hauled, Shani down the soft, dirt-like ramp into the Drath base. They didn't go far. Shani sent Narcisse back up to get Tracey out of the transport once Shani was at the base of the ramp.

The lights were off, only occasional flickers of what had to be emergency lights along the floor by Shani's feet illuminating her. Payton frowned at her. She sighed and sagged as if all she wanted was to collapse.

"No sitting down," Payton told her.

"We can't..." Shani started. Her voice was still too rough, too much like a growl instead of like normal. "They left. They won't come back."

"Like fuck they won't," Payton said with an amused snort that made xyr ribs scream at xem. "I've met your supervisors, Shani. And their supervisors. Not to mention a couple of your military Drath. They'll leap right at this, fangs bared."

That sent Shani into amused snorting laughs that wrapped her tail into a tight corkscrew despite how tired and sore she had to be. Good. It wasn't like Payton lied. Her people lived for a good fight, and this was one at a level that Payton could barely wrap xyr head around.

"We've got incoming," Narcisse shouted as she came running back from the transport with Tracey over her shoulder and a blaster tucked into the back of her pants.

"Told you they'd come," Payton said. Xe jerked xyr chin towards Shani. "Go. Get both of them to the medical bay. I'll hold here."

"You'll get your broken ribs into the base, down that ramp and let the door seal," Narcisse countered with a scowl that bared her fangs and made her eyes narrow enticingly.

Well, threateningly, but Payton couldn't help but find it enticing when Narcisse got all vicious and deadly. Nothing sexier than competence and deadly skill mixed up in the same person. Still strange for a non-Gensyn to be sexy but Payton was tired and sore enough to admit it right now when xe wouldn't have any other time.

"Stop flirting and move your ass," Narcisse huffed as a blush swept over her cheeks.

And Payton had forgotten Narcisse's nose again, damn it. So much for privately acknowledging that xe found her attractive. There were no secrets at all around Narcisse, Tracey or Shani.

Not that it mattered as the sound of flyers came over the top of the surrounding fern trees. Lots of flyers. Way too many of them.

There was a rumble underneath that sound that reminded Payton of the sea aliens and their unnatural tsunami. All right then. Into the base and hopefully they wouldn't get drowned before they could do a damned thing.

Payton jerked xyr chin for Narcisse to go first. Xe waited for her to haul Tracey down the slope, then followed her down. The instant xyr boots left the ramp, the ground slid upwards smoothly. They were left standing in a dark hallway with low, flickering lights along the walls, with no way to go anywhere but onwards.

The med bay was only about ten meters up the hallway, off on the right. Shani staggered in and then collapsed into a low hollow dug into the earthy ground. Lights gleamed around her. Nowhere else. Which, actually, made a great deal of sense in Payton's exhausted mind.

Why light things when eyes weren't the way Drath interacted with the world? They used their noses. Light would just distract them from the scents.

"Okay, I have Tracey on the path to waking up," Narcisse announced from her spot kneeling next to another hollow in the ground. Tracey lay twitching inside of it, more violently than she had before. "You need to sit down and rest, Payton. The smell of water is rising. The Women of the Sea are here and they're going to tear their way into the base by pure force. We don't have time for you to be sick."

"I need fluids and something to eat," Payton said as xe slid down the wall and sat with a tired sigh. "Any fluids, any food. Anything organic, actually."

"On it," Narcisse promised before running out of the med bay and up the dim hallways.

Payton shook xyr head before turning to Shani. "Can you contact your people from there?"

"Already did," Shani said. Her ears weren't as tight against her skull as before, but she still looked like she felt terrible. "The system is having a hard time breaking these things. I won't... be much good in a fight."

"Shani," Payton said with a little snort-laugh that made xem wince, "you never were. That's why you had Gensyn guards. Seriously, from now on you're going nowhere without Drath guards. Too much of a trouble magnet."

Shani's tail curled in loose loops as she chuckled, jaw dropped open and ears relaxing a touch. "I won't argue it anymore. This has been... horrid. Mostly."

"She is amazing, isn't she?" Payton agreed. Xe didn't need to smell as well as Shani what the "mostly" referred to. "Both of them are."

"Narcisse is... more," Shani said.

Shani's amusement faded into tight-lipped fear and trembling worry. She set her nose against the floor, shut her eyes and shook for a good while. Payton wanted to go over and pet her the way Narcisse would.

Xe wasn't getting up, though. Not without a hand.

Then Narcisse ran back in with six of the soft-bodied fist-sized balls that Drath used as water containers in a small net bag, and about twenty packs of food in the hard-sided Drath containers that were as edible as their contents.

"I don't know what they are," Narcisse said as she passed Payton the packs of food, "but they smell like meat mixed with some sort of vegetables."

"Good enough," Payton said as xe tore one open and set to work shoving it into xyr mouth.

"Uh..."

"Don't worry, Gensyn really can eat anything we can eat," Shani reassured Narcisse. "The Women of the Sea are here. The security system is going nuts."

The ravening hunger that had Payton eating like a starving animal didn't stop xem from frowning at Shani. Xe didn't hear anything. Or see any sign of warnings. Narcisse, on the other hand, rubbed her nose as if something really pungent was bothering her.

"I know," Narcisse agreed. "Just worried. All right, I need weapons I can use against those... people. Walk me through getting into the system here, Shani."

She marched over to the area next to Shani, crouching down to set her hands on a spot that looked no different from anything else to Payton. Xe shrugged and went back to eating. There was a battle coming. Xe needed to give xyr body as much fuel as possible so that xe could actually help in the fight.

If possible.

Xe wasn't sure exactly what xe could do against sea aliens surrounded by bubbles of water that they controlled absolutely. All the weapons that Payton had were worthless against water. Hopefully, not that Payton really believed it down deep, Narcisse would come up with something new and dangerous that xe could actually use.

Sure hoped so. Being able to turn the tides and fight properly instead of just running would be a nice change. Payton shook xyr head as xe crunched the third container and chewed it up while ripping the fourth open.

Food first. Then water. Then fighting.

At least they'd made it to the base, at last. All they had to do was survive long enough for Shani's people to come for her. Everything else could wait until after that.

TWENTY-THREE
FOR BLOOD AND FRIENDSHIP

THE AIR SMELLED of sea salt. Stank of it. Narcisse wanted to rub her nose, to sneeze until the salt-stench was driven out. No point to trying though.

The sea salt smell came from above them, seeping downward through the earth and armor of the Drath base. Narcisse didn't know just how much armor there was between them and the Women of the Sea. Hopefully it was enough to keep them from being drowned outright, but she wouldn't guarantee it. Water was…

…unstoppable. Catastrophic. Terrifyingly powerful. The thick, rising smell of sea-salt tangled with the angry fractured grammar of the Women of the Sea in the back of Narcisse's mind was a nightmare. One that she would likely remember in actual dreams for years to come.

If they survived, of course.

The sea-salt stench also came from Shani whose body was a battle-ground between the Women of the Sea and the Drath technology, neither of which Narcisse could affect.

Not properly. Her fingers weren't the right shape to work the controls that Shani tried to explain in scents and little nudges with her tail-hand. There were things that Narcisse should be doing that she literally couldn't understand. Her nose, her brain, didn't have the capacity to scent them properly.

Which wouldn't stop Narcisse from trying until she managed something.

"No, not that," Shani growled, tired and low and smelling of despair.

"I hate this," Narcisse sang as she reached over and petted Shani despite the horrible things parasiting her strength and energy. "I hate this so very, very much! I want it to stop. I want it to fall off you. I want it to die, die, die."

She didn't sing it to Shani. No point to that when Shani could smell the emotions and thoughts on Narcisse's skin. Narcisse sang to the Women of the Sea complaining about too much earth between them and their target. She sang it to the horrible biological machines hurting Shani.

Powder rose up off Shani, drifting up into the air like ash from a bonfire. It wasn't a small cloud. It was a huge, terrifying cloud that made Payton squawk as xe scrambled against the wall, trying to stand. Narcisse kept right on thinking "die, die, die" at the Women of the Sea, at their horrible little machine-parasites or whatever they were.

Shani gasped and slapped her forepaws against the floor just outside of her hospital bed-hollow. "Don't stop!"

"Won't," Narcisse promised as she bend her head and pressed her forehead against Shani's neck.

Let the damned things infect her instead of Shani, except no, don't. They needed to leave her Shani alone. They needed to go away. They needed to—

A bitter almond warning scent filled the infirmary as a competing cloud of silver mist came out of the ceiling. It flowed down, capturing the rising ashes of the Women of the Sea's parasites, then it soaked both Narcisse and Shani.

It felt a little like having mercury flow over her clean room gloves, slick and metallic and cold. The mist formed into a film that curled over Narcisse, briefly covering her eyes and nose and mouth. Then it swept over Shani, stripping her fur clean and leaving her gasping and shaking in the bed-hollow.

"What the fuck was that?" Payton snarled as xe finally got to xyr feet.

"Security system," Shani said through chattering teeth and whimpering growls deep in her chest. "Narcisse, you, you broke their hold. You reprogrammed them."

"How the fuck did you do that?" Payton asked in the exact same tone.

Xe slid back down the wall to stare at Narcisse as if she'd grown a second head. She stared back at xem, blinking to keep her eyes from crossing. The headache was back. So very back. And so very bad, too.

Her head felt like the top was about to come off. It felt like something was slicing its way out from the inside, sawing through bone and flesh as it broke for freedom.

"Crap," Payton said as Shani grabbed Narcisse and shoved her down into the surprisingly comfy bed-hollow. "Is she dying? We can't afford for her to die right now."

"Coming close to it," Shani said as she worked the invisible controls on the bed. "Stay with us, Narcisse. Don't pass out. The med system isn't used to humans."

"Ow." Narcisse winced and spoke quieter. "So much ow. Something to keep my blood pressure from spiking would be good. And to keep my blood vessels from bursting. Oh, and a broad-spectrum pain killer, please."

Shani wheeze-laughed as she programed exactly that into the system.

Another silvery cloud of stuff came down from the ceiling. Not in a cloud, actually, but in a long stream that settled like the finest silk thread over Narcisse's head. She didn't feel anything. Not hot, not cold, just the faintest sensation of touch and then the pain abruptly began to ease.

Oh, that was nice. Even better, her heart stopped pounding like it was going to go straight through her ribcage. Trying to run away with her brain. Hopefully they would both stay where they belonged now.

"I think the pain killers might be a bit too strong," Payton commented from somewhere near orbit.

When had xe gone so far away?

"Working on it," Shani replied.

She sounded like she was right next to Narcisse's ear. When Narcisse managed to slowly roll her head to the right, there Shani was, nose pressed right against Narcisse's face. Narcisse smiled and pressed a tiny kiss against Shani's nose.

"Favorite person," Narcisse said.

The words came out all mushy and strange. Narcisse frowned. So did Shani as she worked the controls. A few moments later, Narcisse's head went as clear as a winter morning over the ridges back home when there wasn't a single cloud in the sky and the air was so cold that your breath crystalized in front of you as you hunted.

"Wow, that was weird," Narcisse said. "Effective, but weird."

"Can you still hear them?" Payton asked. Xe looked very intent. Also very wary, which Narcisse grinned over, but definitely very intent.

"Mhm," Narcisse confirmed. "I can. They're still trying to get through the armor. The salt smell is gone, though. I thought they were tearing through to get at us, but it must have been the things attacking you, Shani."

Narcisse moved to sit up, but Shani's tail-hand descended to press Narcisse back into the bed-hollow. It was rather more comfortable than Narcisse would have expected. She stayed there, breathing in Shani's worry and the oddly metallic smell of the Drath nanites.

What else could they be, really? Shani might not be able to say that the silvery thread connected to Narcisse's forehead was a nanite supply going in to fix her poor abused brain, but they obviously had to be something like that.

More advanced that human nanites. They'd almost have to be given that the Drath had been technologically advanced for millions of years, longer than humans even existed. Narcisse frowned at Shani.

"Will you be able to help Tracey, too?" Narcisse asked.

"The bed says that she's healing nicely on her own," Shani replied.

Her scent added on that Tracey actually was doing quite well and would wake up in about fifteen minutes or so, hungry, cranky and looking for the food that Payton had already consumed.

"Save one of the food packs for Tracey," Narcisse told Payton since xe couldn't smell the scent-conversation. "She'll be really grumpy if she wakes up with nothing to eat."

Payton paused in the process of opening one of the few remaining food packs. "Oh. Right. Sorry. You three are probably hungry, too."

"Oh, one each should be plenty," Narcisse said. "Neither Tracey nor I will want to eat a ton. It would weigh us down right before a battle."

The problem was that the Women of the Sea were making triumphant dolphin squeaks colored with acid green and neon yellow excitement. They'd figured out the lock on the entry tunnel. Well, they'd figured out where it was and that it was a door, not how to unlock it.

Narcisse patted Shani and sat up.

"They found the door and they'll break the lock shortly," Narcisse said. "Shani, can you get up and fight them?"

"Not... really," Shani admitted with a shameful curl of musky dismay. "I'm a researcher, not a warrior. I mean, I could set off the automatic defenses, but they'll go after the three of you, too. I can't let that happen."

Narcisse nodded. "Then get on your comms and tell your people to get their tails down here. If you can give me some sort of interface, Payton and I will hold the line until Tracey wakes up. If we have to, how deep can we retreat into the base? Are there successive doors we can shut to keep the Women of the Sea out?"

"...Probably?" Shani said, ears sliding back towards her skull as her eyes went wide and her tail anxiously twisted itself into worried knots. "I never paid attention to stuff like that before."

"Get the medical systems to wake Tracey up," Narcisse said with a sigh. "Interface for me, weapons for Payton. Tracey will help you figure out the security system and call your people."

The nanites flowed over Narcisse's hands, forming a silvery film over her fingers and palms. Then a second thread of silvery nanites came down to drift delicately over Tracey's forehead while Payton dragged xemself up to xyr feet.

Narcisse wolfed down one of the food packets, barely tasting the meat-like gel and the crunchy cuts of some sort of succulent that she'd never seen before. The water was water, though it was fun to bite down on the little bubbles and feel them burst in her mouth. Quite nice, even. Better than drinking from a bottle, that was certain.

They set up just outside of the doorway to the infirmary, Payton lying on the floor and sighting xyr blaster up the hallway and up the ramp. Xe frowned at xyr rifle and then turned to Narcisse.

"I won't be much good," Payton admitted as if it hurt xem to say it. "None of my weapons work with water. The surface tension..."

"I know," Narcisse agreed. "But what else can we do?"

She crouched down and set one hand on the control pad built into the floor next to the wall. It wasn't much of anything. There were no switches or anything really visible. Narcisse smelled it more than saw it, a slight depression filled with the scents of a hundred different Drath checking the security system and then trotting onwards during their patrol route through the base.

Her nanite glove vibrated against Narcisse's palm at the same instant a terrifying groan echoed overhead.

"They've got the door," Narcisse announced loudly for Shani's sake. "I give it one minute, maybe two before they tear it open."

"And then we drown," Payton murmured just quietly enough that Narcisse didn't feel like she had to reply.

Xe weren't wrong. The security system sent up showers of warning scents, acrid smoke scent that meant something about running now mixed with citrus so strong that Shani sneezed and Tracey groaned. The citrus seemed to be warning that it was an invasion, which, thank you, they already knew.

Narcisse turned that particular warning down and set to work trying to get the security system to close pressure doors. Lock the base down. Give them bubbles full of air so that they wouldn't drown. Anything that would keep the four of them from dying.

"I'm up!" Tracey squawked. "What the fuck? Ow, ow, ow, oh... huh. Wow, that's some serious pain killers."

"Escape route and pressure doors," Narcisse called to Tracey. "Call the Drath down, Tracey!"

"Oh, right, on it," Tracey replied.

Narcisse heard her scramble out of the bed-hollow and turned back to the security system which absolutely did not have anything like pressure doors or bubbles that would keep them alive. There weren't even lower levels that they could flee to. The security system refused to allow mere humans to go deeper than they'd already gone.

Shani didn't have the authority to give them clearance.

Which meant that the creaks and groans of the entrance ramp and rising scent of salt water in the air meant that they were going to die. All four of them.

"This won't work," Narcisse huffed. "There's got to be something that we can do! I mean, I've got those stupid Women in my head. I can't just yell at them to go away."

Although...

...Narcisse had made the junior Women of the Sea let the yacht go.

She couldn't use the Drath technology.

Maybe she could use the Women of the Sea's technology against them. It was worth a try, anyway. What did she have to lose? Their lives were already forfeit.

"Shani, get them down here as quickly as possible and get a pain killer feed on me," Narcisse shouted over the scream of the entrance ramp being slowly forced open.

Shani scrambled in with a silvery balloon on a thin gossamer string. She reared up and attached it to the back of Narcisse's neck. Narcisse nodded, patted Shani, and then sent her back in to help Tracey with the comms and security system.

Then Narcisse strode forward to the end of the ramp even though Payton screamed at her not to be an idiot.

It wasn't idiocy if it worked.

Narcisse was the only one here who could make it work.

She wouldn't fail Shani.

Ever.

No matter what it cost.

As the ramp shuddered and fell in to the open position, water rushed down into the Drath base. Straight at Narcisse. She could see it, feel the Women of the Sea, their organic technology that glimmered like phosphorescent plankton in the dark wave of water rushing at her face.

Narcisse held up her silver-coated hands and screamed.

"No!"

TWENTY-FOUR
DEATH'S MANY FORMS

PAYTON BELLOWED AS XE FIRED into the churning mass of water barreling straight at Narcisse. What the ever-loving fuck was wrong with her? Xe couldn't hear what she yelled at the sea aliens, but what the fuck did she think that would...

...do?

The water slammed into a wall. An invisible wall.

No! No, the water *became* a wall, right there a bare centimeter from Narcisse's palms.

The roar of the water and scream of tortured metal died into a burbling stream of water that seeped around the edges of Narcisse's wall. Then the seepage reversed course and rejoined with her wall.

"How the fuck are you doing that?" Payton asked in a scratchy whisper that felt louder than xyr loudest bellow.

"Focus," Narcisse said between her teeth. She didn't look Payton's way. "Determination. I. Promised. Shani. Won't fail her. I won't!"

Payton shuddered as squid-like... things... appeared on the other side of Narcisse's water wall. Their many arms squirmed in Payton's mind. Xe could taste colors. See sounds that xe'd never even imagined before. The words, if those were words, drove Payton to bury xyr face in the dirt.

Blaster hilt.

Xyr blaster.

Fucking aliens!

Payton gritted xyr teeth as xe raised xyr head. Yep, the aliens were just as mind-bending as before. Xe still lifted xyr blaster and fired towards Narcisse's wall of water.

The blast splattered on the water wall. Narcisse barked a laugh. Behind her wall, the sea aliens opened beak-like mouths and screamed. The sound cut through Payton's head.

Xe fired again.

This time the bolt went through the wall. It refracted inside the water, useless, harmless, pointless.

The sea aliens screamed higher, louder. They jetted away from Narcisse and Payton so Payton fired again and again. Xyr blaster bolts made the water shimmer and dance. It quivered like gelatin under a little kid's fascinated pokes.

"Stop," Narcisse told Payton.

Xe did.

"Why?" Payton asked.

"You're killing whatever's in the water that lets me control it," Narcisse explained. "Or they're pulling it back."

"Tracey, get the damned pressure walls down!" Payton bellowed over xyr shoulder.

"We're working on it!" Tracey shouted back. "Stupid system is fighting us."

"Imminent flood warning," Payton shouted as xe scrambled to xyr feet, stowing weapons as xe went. "Like, immanent!"

Xe grabbed Narcisse by the waist. The water wall was more like a blob of gelatin slowly flowing down the ramp towards them. Narcisse panted, hands still out and teeth gritted. Payton picked her up and ran towards the infirmary door.

"Down!" Tracey shouted as she dashed past Payton.

Shani flashed by, too.

Payton hefted Narcisse up on xyr shoulder and ran for all xe was worth. Too much damned running on this stupid mission. Xe hadn't run this much since xe was a kid back on xyr home station.

Xe had never run like this though.

The water rumbled forward in jerks and starts. Payton didn't look over xyr shoulder as xe pounded after the tip of Shani's tail. It was a dim ghost in the dark tunnels. Thank fuck the Drath were as tall as a human at the shoulder. If they were the size of the dogs they so resembled, Payton would've had to crawl.

And then xe would've been dead.

Along with Narcisse. Tracey. Shani.

"Can't hold it much longer," Narcisse wheezed.

"Tracey!" Payton bellowed.

"Hoof it!" Tracey yelled back at xem.

Payton ran harder. Xyr newly healed ribcage screamed with pain. Xe ignored it. Narcisse whimpered over xyr shoulder. Payton ignored that, too.

Sweat dripped into xyr eyes. When xe blinked it away, xe nearly ran smack into a wall. Tracey reached around it to grab Narcisse off Payton's shoulder.

"Inside," Tracey ordered.

Payton shoved Narcisse in, then collapsed into the dark hollow with some wheezing of xyr own. The wall closed behind Payton, smacking xem on xyr butt. At the same moment, the roar of water erupted as Narcisse lost control.

Or the sea aliens won.

Didn't matter.

What mattered was their hideaway. Big enough to have sufficient air? Armored enough to take the weight of the water? Any way to communicate with the Drath?

"Yes, maybe and hopefully," Shani said.

A stink of musk filled the air and then lights bloomed in the floor. The entire floor, that is. Whole thing lit up like it was made of glass backed by lights instead of dirt.

Their little room was about six meters in diameter, a perfect circle. The ceiling was only a few centimeters over Payton's head. Dirt walls, glowing dirt floor, spot in the middle that was hollowed out like the infirmary beds. Shani crouched there, stubby finger-toes digging into the glowing dirt as her tail manipulated something in the dirt beside her right hip.

"They're so mad," Narcisse whispered as she rocked, hands wrapped around her head. "So mad. They hate that I could do that. Hate it! "

"Why?" Payton asked.

Xe didn't sit down like Tracey did. Certainly didn't wrap an arm around Narcisse's shoulders. Xe did reload xyr blaster and make sure that xe had full clips in everything xe still had. Pity there wasn't more food. The other three needed to eat. Payton was good for the moment. Xyr body would heal entirely in a couple more minutes.

As long as the sea aliens didn't smash their way into their hideout.

"They won't," Shani promised.

"We're animals," Narcisse said at the same time. "That's what they think. Humans, all of us, are animals. We can't think. We can't, can't use real technology. It's got to be a fluke. I can't have done it deliberately. Intelligently."

Tracey snorted. "As if. They're idiots if they think that."

"No," Narcisse said, licking her lips and staring up at Payton, then at Shani. "They're not. They're even more xenophobic than humanity is."

"All the races are more xenophobic than humanity," Shani commented with a grimace as the stink of urine and chocolate filled the room. "Including us. You guys are bizarrely social compared to every other intelligent species in the galaxy. There is no one else who makes friends like you do."

Payton opened xyr mouth to protest that humans were the exact opposite of social. How many billions of humans had died in stupid wars over their history? But yeah, they hadn't exactly stayed safe on their home world. Narcisse, all by herself, proved that to be a lie.

"Thank you," Narcisse said. She grinned at Payton even though her eyes were visibly dilated differently. "We have to fight them, Shani. They will break through. They've already figured out how to get through the pressure doors to the lower levels."

Shani growled, not meeting anyone's eyes. "I know. High Command is going to be so furious about this."

"We need weapons and a way to breathe when the water gets in," Payton said. "Armor to protect us somehow. Tracey and I have to be able to fight, too. Can the silvery threads you made help?"

"I'm on it," Tracey exclaimed with delight. "Sit there and rest, Narcisse. Payton, I'll need help. I don't have the training for that."

"I do," Narcisse complained.

She subsided with a grimace when Payton glared at her. Pouting at Tracey got her even more glares, this time from both Tracey and Shani. Not that it mattered as Tracey started working with the Drath tech off on one side of their shelter.

"Armor won't work," Narcisse commented as if she was observing the sun rising and thought it was nice. "They can control the pressure of the water. What you need is something that will negate the biologics in the water that are the base of their technology."

Payton turned to stare at Narcisse. Her eyes were locked on Shani who blinked back at her, ears rotating like satellites. Okay. Right.

"Breathing is still an issue," Payton said in as mild a tone as xe could manage. "So is seeing."

"Mask that converts water into gasses and goggles that have infrared and all," Narcisse countered.

"Flippers?" Payton suggested with a wave to Tracey to get to work doing what Narcisse had suggested.

She might be half out of her mind from the pain and the sea aliens shouting in her head, but she wasn't wrong. Not wrong at all. Especially given the way she'd held their water back.

"Wouldn't hurt but honestly, I want to keep the water out," Narcisse said. "Kill the biologics, stop the water. Stop them. Should work."

"I can work with that," Shani said, ears perking up and hind end wiggling with excitement.

"So can I," Tracey said just as excitedly. "Though I think we need some sort of weapon."

Payton hummed and pulled xyr blaster out, studying it. "I was killing the biologics, wasn't I? That's why the wall started wobbling when I was firing into it."

"Oh, yes," Narcisse said. "I let the blasts into the water and then the blast refracted inside the water, killing the biologics. That was lovely."

Her grin was a fanged, vicious thing that showed just how much of a predator she actually was. Payton licked xyr lips. In any other circumstances, xe would've already gone in for a kiss. Fuck if xe wasn't tempted to do it anyway. Only not. The other three could smell xyr arousal and that was just embarrassing. Xe hadn't been that obvious about getting excited since xe was a teen.

Tracey snort-laughed. "Trust me, you're painfully obvious."

"I like it," Narcisse said loftily even though her cheeks had gone red. "I mean, not now. We've got aliens to kill and Shani to save. The Drath High Command needs to know about all of this. But later, maybe. I mean, this vacation is completely shot but there's no reason not to have a proper fling once we're free and not dead."

"Hooray we didn't die sex is always good," Tracey agreed while Shani's tail went into a tight corkscrew and her sides shook with laughter.

"Mark that on the agenda, then," Payton said. Xe turned back to Tracey who passed up a thin silver membrane. "Mask?"

"Full face," Tracey agreed. "Should cover your ears, too, which will let us communicate even under water."

Shani's mask was more like a cone, but it worked perfectly for her. There were collar-like strips of silvery stuff around their necks that should, hopefully, keep the biologics in the water from getting too close. And then Tracey and Payton got down to engineering more silvery film things that would transform the blaster bolts going through them into broad-spectrum biologic killers.

Might not hurt the sea aliens themselves, but if Payton could kill their tech, xe could keep Shani safe.

Xe could keep all four of them alive.

And that was what mattered.

Everything else could wait.

Payton helped Narcisse back to her feet, one arm wrapped around her waist because she was still unsteady. Not helpless. Never that. But unsteady enough that Payton supported her with one arm and aimed xyr modified weapon with the other as the pressure door creaked warningly.

More silvery things wrapped their feet, glueing them to the floor in ways that seemed more like they'd been fused to the floor than like magnetic boots or cleats on the soles of their shoes. Which was fine. Anchored or not, the fucking waiting was over.

Here they go.

Time to fight.

TWENTY-FIVE
CHOICES MADE AND ACCEPTED

THERE WAS NOWHERE to go from here. Narcisse didn't need to ask Shani to know that. She could smell it in the air which didn't flow onwards but stayed circling around them. It rumbled in the layers upon layers of scents on the floor that told of people, Drath, coming in, circling the room, leaving by the same door.

This room had one way in.

One way out.

And the Women of the Sea loomed in all their mind-breaking horror on the far side of the door with all their nasty biological technology. Narcisse had the scent of it now. The sea salt smell was distinctive. Thinking back to when they'd met Shani, Narcisse had smelled it even then.

She'd put it down to the ocean outside, but it had radiated up off Shani as if she'd been swimming in the ocean.

None of them were swimming now with the ocean so far away but the sea salt stink filled their.

Shani's scent spiked cinnamon excitement and bitter almond desperation. "They're sending the warship down!"

"You have a warship in system?" Payton asked furiously though xe kept xyr eyes and gun focused on the door. "Since when?"

The scents pouring up off the comm system on the floor under Shani's feet went so thick that Tracey sneezed. Narcisse wanted to but she wouldn't allow her focus to break, not now. The communication was so dense with information that it smelled more like a musk-oil perfume mixed with thiol stink.

It coated the back of Narcisse's throat, filled her nose to the point that the rising smell of sea salt receded. Not all the way, just enough that Narcisse had to cough to clear her nose.

"Since about half an hour ago," Shani said, sides shaking and tail in lazy loops of exhausted laughter. "The High Command really is ready to bite everyone between them and me. They, they're mad. So mad. This is a war."

"Yes," Narcisse agreed, focusing on the Women of the Sea's rising fury and desperation. "It is. And they won't let us go if they can help it. We saw too much. They want there to be plausible deniability."

"For this?" Payton huffed. "Not a chance."

Conversation ceased as the door creaked dramatically. Narcisse could hear the Women of the Sea above ground shouting down to the young ones outside the door.

"Be ready!" Narcisse shouted over the scream of the bending metal.

Water rushed in at them, a dark, foaming wall filled with death. The onrush of it surged around Narcisse's knees, sucking at her ankles. Only Payton's grip on Narcisse's waist kept her upright.

The water poured in so fast that in the time it took for the door to crash against the back wall, the water went from knee height to chest height.

"Still outside," Narcisse said.

The water rushed up over their heads by the time she got the words out.

In the darkness of the Drath burrow with only a few dim, blinking emergency lights, the Women of the Sea became spotlights. Torches. Blazing suns with wiggling tentacles and saucer-sized eyes that stared, hard and cold, at Narcisse, Payton, Tracey and especially at Shani.

"Now," Narcisse ordered.

Both Payton and Tracey fired their guns.

Instead of a minor and wobbly effect on the biological whatevers the Women of the Sea had flooded the water with, the newly adjusted guns sent out a pulse that made the junior Women of the Sea flare neon bright and then jet away up towards the surface.

In clouds of ink, no less.

The water around them turned into a supernova of light, tiny explosions making the water foam and heat like they were inside of a tea kettle reaching a boil. Payton fired again and again, methodically working xyr way towards filling the room with so much energy that the water turned to literal steam around them.

"On the ground!" Shani shouted.

Narcisse hauled at Payton's shoulder as she let her knees bend after the trembling effort of staying upright with her head hurting this much. Payton collapsed to the ground, still firing.

"What the hell?" Tracey spluttered. "We're going to boil!"

"No," Shani said. "We won't. The warship is overhead. They're going to start firing soon."

The attacking Women of the Sea raged in streaks of purple fury that tasted of rotted cabbage. All except on up on the surface who flared magnesium bright in Narcisse's head. She keened as blood bloomed on the back of her throat.

Eliminate / wash away / retreat immediately.

"Clear the room of their tech, Tracey!" Narcisse shouted as mind-warping order echoed through the Women of the Sea clustered outside of the room. "They're going nuclear on us!"

Or whatever it was when you had a soup full of nanites surrounding you ordered to disassemble you at all costs.

Both Tracey and Payton fired indiscriminately, not aiming, not thinking, no pause between shots. Narcisse gritted her teeth and shouted at the Women of the Sea's tech in the room, in the base, here on land.

"Off! Off! Off!" Narcisse bellowed at it all.

There was blood in her throat. Dripping out of her ears. Even the pain control device that Shani had given Narcisse didn't suffice to keep her head from splitting and her eyes from screwing shut in agony.

"Off!" Narcisse said, gasped, gasped again and then howled as something exploded.

Not the white nothing concussive force of the orbital strike.

Not a grenade going off with shrapnel whipping past her ears.

Explosions of rotted apple and overcooked cabbage. Explosions of sound so quiet that it made the silence echo. Explosions of pressed all across her arms and hands and legs and back and stomach but not on her face where the blood had coated her breathing mask.

Her blood.

Oh.

That's not good.

Narcisse rocked with the shaking of the cold, wet world, limp as an overcooked noodle about to fall to bits if it was touched. Felt rather like she'd been cooked too long, too. It was…

…somewhat worrying, actually.

Was this what brain death felt like as it happened?

Or maybe it was a seizure?

Abruptly, the water surrounding Narcisse drained away.

She flopped to the muddy floor and lay there, panting. The silence in her head was…

Worrying?

A relief?

It was there and it was odd after so long with the rumble and grumble of the Women of the Seal cutting slivers of her hindbrain away. A hand grabbed Narcisse's shoulder. Another hand ripped the breathing mask off.

Oh, much better. Narcisse coughed, spraying blood across Payton's face. Chest. Hand that reached out to brush something wet and nasty off her face. Blood clots. Oh, very not good. Her nanites shouldn't have allowed that.

"I've got her," Payton said to someone over xyr shoulder. "She's alive."

"Thank fuck," Tracey whined. "Worst vacation ever. Well. This part has been. The rest was kind of amazing, honestly. What a great hunt. Nothing is ever going to top it."

Narcisse's ribs laughed without notifying her that they found Tracey funny. That didn't hurt but wow, the shaking made her poor head feel like she had a little man with a very big sledgehammer pounding away as he tried to escape her skull.

"Well done," Shani said as she cuddled up next to Narcisse and wrapped that marvelously sinuous tail around her. "Come on, child. Cuddle up and rest. You did well. They're gone. Just rest with me."

"What… happened?" Narcisse managed to say.

The words came out horribly mushy, but Payton obviously understood them because xe frowned and turned to Tracey who leaned on xyr shoulder while looking generally exhausted, drenched and so jittery that she wouldn't be sleeping for at least a day or two.

Tracey was always that way after the big hunts. Where Narcisse crashed and slept like the dead, Tracey kept going for another day minimum before she calmed down enough to recuperate.

"We were firing, and it wasn't doing much good," Tracey said, pulling her breathing mask off and blowing out a long, hard sigh as it crumbled to dust in her hand. "More waves of the little glittery things kept coming. I could see those squid-ladies off up the hallway. They flared bright, then faded, flared and faded. Every time one of them flared, another glittery wave came at us."

Payton nodded, grim and determined and alert even now. "Every time the wave entered the room, it fell apart. Shattered, broken, whatever. Each wave got further. When you screamed, all the waves blinked out. That final scream matched up with some… something."

"My people activated the defenses," Shani said, rubbing Narcisse's tummy like she was a baby who needed to be soothed to sleep. "You shut off the waves coming at us. The defenses… killed the Women of the Sea in here. The one on the surface jetted away. My people are hunting her, though I doubt they'll catch her. You did good, Narcisse. You also badly damaged your brain, so please, rest."

"Good idea," Narcisse said.

Mumbled.

She rested her head on Shani's foreleg and let her body go lax.

They'd done it. They'd saved Shani. Started a war in the process, but well, that apparently had been brewing for a long, long time.

A war between alien species for… what?

That was the real question, wasn't it? What did the Women of the Sea want from this war? What did the Drath want?

And what would happen to humanity on all their worlds in all their many, varied forms?

Humans adapted to most everything. They'd lived through wars and death back on Old Earth, lived through more limited wars now on their various worlds. In one way this war wasn't going to be anything new.

Except that this time Narcisse was a weapon against the Women of the Sea.

This time the war was being fought around them, over their heads because humanity as a whole were children compared to the other intelligent space-faring races.

"I can see you thinking too hard," Tracey commented.

"Can't sleep," Narcisse admitted and then chuckled at Shani's tail-hand rubbing her belly again. "Too much adrenaline. And my head is so very quiet. No murmurs at all. I didn't realize that I was… hearing? Hearing works. I didn't realize I was hearing the Women of the Sea practically from the moment we arrived on planet. Now they're gone."

Great bounding splashes sounded from outside their room. Barks and growls echoed. Shani's sent brightened, lightened, filled with hope and a sort of papery resignation that probably meant that there were a million forms for her to fill out now.

"They're gone," Narcisse repeated because she didn't think that even Shani got it. "I think the Women of the Sea fled somehow. I don't know that any of them are still on-planet."

"Oh," Shani breathed. "Well, that's a problem for someone else to deal with. Like Rrutia. She can handle it. I'm too old for that sort of nonsense."

"Seriously?" a new Drath growled from the doorway. "You're going to dump this whole mess on… what is wrong with her face?"

"I can hear them," Narcisse said without opening her eyes. The scents were enough to go by. She didn't need her eyes for this. "And interface successfully with their technology. It just hurts to do it."

Narcisse knew perfectly well that her scent caried the knowledge that she was a weapon against the Women of the Sea even if her words didn't convey it. From the way Tracey bit off a curse and Shani sighed, they got it.

"Humans are a threat to the Women of the Sea," Payton said, xyr voice so close and so fierce that Narcisse actually did open her eyes. Xe stared at Narcisse, not at Rrutia or Tracey or Shani. "Even those of us who can't do what Narcisse did are a threat. They spent way too much time and effort controlling everyone for us not to be dangerous to them."

The silence echoed as a flood of bitter almond worry and bright citrus hope flooded off both Shani and Rrutia. The splashing of paws outside the room brought wet hints of curiosity, scientific interest and pure annoyance at the mess to be cleaned up.

"They're mine," Shani said to Rrutia. "Especially Narcisse, but Tracey and Payton, too. They chose me. They promised to keep me safe and get me home when I could barely move for being so sick from the Women of the Sea's attack. They're mine and I'm keeping them."

Rrutia whined and snapped her jaws at Shani. "Fine. The four of you are being evacuated. I'll ask questions… later. Go."

Several Drath, smaller and more delicate, rushed in with floating beds that they swiftly loaded Shani and Narcisse onto. Shani flopped on her floating bed and closed her eyes with the sort of exhausted finality that Narcisse had seen on Mother after the worst hunts.

Over. It was over and now Shani could rest.

Narcisse smiled as Payton patted her hip and Tracey gave Narcisse a thumb's up. It really was over. She shut her eyes and let sleep capture her. She'd kept her promise at last.#

AUTHOR'S NOTE: CRADLE OF THE DAY

I COULDN'T LEAVE *this book without sharing a sample of the previous book, Cradle of the Day. It's just as much part of the opening of the war, just in those earliest stages where everyone's twitching and highly aware that something's gone very, very wrong.*

Well, not everyone. Ale knows. Her whole life has just been overturned and there's nothing to do but cope with it as an entire galaxy lands right on her head. Eka knows, too, but xe's facing a whole different prospect than Ale. Until they crash right into each other and then attract the attention of the Drath.

And the people aiming to knock the Drath out of their ruling position over Galactic civilization.

Hope you enjoy the sample!

1. EAGER EYES

ALE SLOWED, stopped, stared out the viewport at the stars. So many stars. After living her whole live in the Hexal City's Undercity on Melin, seeing stars would always be a thing of wonder. She ran her fingertips over the viewport. No cold, not even a chill, but that was to be expected. There were layers upon layers of steel, insulation and machinery between her and the stars. This was, she had been told, not an actual window. Just a viewscreen so that occupants of the *Graceful Swan* didn't feel quite so entombed all the time.

Strange that anyone would mind that feeling.

Voices echoed up the hallway, Seong and Munashe arguing about something. Since Ale met them three months ago, they had never once stopped arguing. If it wasn't the food, it was the pay. If it wasn't the pay, it was their bosses. If it wasn't their bosses, it was their coworkers. Or each other. Or sometimes, just the smell of the air.

Ale wondered, again, as they appeared around the corner whether Ceelen noses were that much more sensitive than hers for all she smelled was the faint grass-like smell of the wall coverings and the hints of her rich stew lunch.

Certainly, she was never going to get used to the clothes the Ceelen wore. Bright colors, bold patterns and flowing fabric that would be so very easy to catch and use against them. Seong's red, gold and black dress had hints of Hyun-Ju styling, wrapping around her torso rather than fitting to it. The sleeves, long and very wide, hinted at Hyun-Ju as well. Odd given that Seong was Melin born and bred, Above, not Undercity. She had the Melin broad, round face with a flat nose rather than the Hyun-Ju narrow nose and angular face.

Munashe was as Ceelen as it was possible to be, tall and muscular with skin as black as the darkness of space. Her ankle-length dress was green and blue, covered with renditions of leaves spotted with holes that Munashe would probably tell Ale were real, not imaginary. Her dreadlocks were so long that they brushed against her ample rear end as she sauntered up the hallway at Seong's side.

"Ah, there you are," Seong said the instant she spotted Ale.

"We were wondering where you'd gotten to after lunch," Munashe agreed. Her eyes swept Ale's body, then she licked her lips. "Looking at the stars again?"

"I paused," Ale said, carefully enunciating her words so that her Undercity accent wouldn't come out in front of these women with their so-different lives and so-beautiful clothes. Shrugged and attempted a smile that went flat almost instantly so she let it go. "I'd thought to explore this level. I don't know the ship well enough yet."

Why that would make Seong and Munashe frown at her, Ale would never understand. One should know one's environment. It was simply logical. Yes, of course, there was little likelihood that Ale would be attacked on the *Graceful Swan*. It was the flagship of the Ceelen and thus very, very safe.

Still.

"Was there new work to do?" Ale asked, clearing her throat and standing a little straighter.

"Ah, no," Seong said, smiling and flapping her hand at Ale. "It's just that King Ru wanted to check in with you, see how you were settling in."

"Apparently," Munashe said with a nod probably intended to be reassuring, "he's doing that with all the Undercity people. He said something about making sure that all 'his kind' were doing okay."

Which, well.

That was reassuring, actually. If anyone understood Ale's difficulties settling in on the *Graceful Swan,* it would be Ru Sashi, former delivery boy turned ruler of the Hyun-Ju and husband to Nthanda Ceelen, ruler of the Ceelen. He was dealing with far more than Ale. He did have twin infants to tend to, with more of them on the way when the baby chambers finally disgorged their contents over the next few years.

"Did he say where to meet him?" Ale asked.

She clenched her hands behind her back, standing straight and tall. As tall as she could be when she was only five and a half foot while wearing boots. Oddly, Munashe bit her lip as if Ale was suddenly striking. Seong's breath caught for a moment as she nodded and gestured for Ale to follow her.

Ale did so.

They ended up in one of the conference rooms that dotted the level three up from where she'd been. This was a level Ale had yet to see but it looked much the same as any other. A faint green stripe along the join between floor and wall instead of the faint purple stripes she was used to on the floors she spent most of her time on.

There was a code there, in the stripes, one that Ale had yet to get brave enough to ask about. Green for command levels? Personal levels? Or just offices, perhaps.

Either way, Ru nodded to her and smirked as he waved Seong and Munashe to leave her with him. He sprawled in his chair at the other end of the small square conference table, one leg draped over the arm of his chair. A comfortable room, barely ten by ten feet, no room for anyone to hide, no cabinets on the walls, just table, chairs, Ru and Ale.

His grin once the door shut was as wicked as Bangers closing in on prey in the deepest levels of the Undercity.

"They're so stuck on you," Ru commented. Then laughed when Ale's jaw dropped open. "For reals, no jokes on you. Stuck like black slime up your nose."

"No." Ale sat opposite him and then shuddered, moving so that she was sitting at ninety degrees to him. Able to watch both him and the door. Much better than leaving her back to the door.

"Hell to the yeah, kiddo," Ru said. He nodded approvingly for her choice of seats. "Most the others keep trying to sit the other side."

"Skin'll crawl into the vents," Ale complained with a shudder.

"No shit," Ru agreed. "Still can't do that. Nthanda doesn't mind. Lets me drape myself over his back."

That made Ale blush so hard that she went lightheaded. A love so strong that your mate trusted you to guard his back. That he offered his body to protect your innards. She couldn't imagine that.

Speaking of.

"They… want me?" Ale asked Ru, allowing her accent to come out fully.

Thick broad vowels and drawled consonants, that's what her first instructor on board had called her accent. A broad one, deep and powerful enough to create a whole new Mellinish language, given a little more time that the Undercity no long had.

"Yeah," Ru said, making a little face, pout of the lips, lift of the eyebrows. He shrugged. "Not sure you're into that. They're bits of fluff. Might want to discourage them if you're not. 'Cause they show no signs of looking anywhere else when you're in the room."

Ale huffed and flicked her fingers at him as if throwing a knife. He grinned, caught the imaginary knife and pretended to balance it on the tip of his finger.

Sassy boy.

Of course, she wanted the security of a mate at her side. The protection. Who wouldn't? But Ale could tell just looking at Seong and Munashe that they were looking for the same. They were not warriors. Not like she and Ru were. Not like Lord Nthanda. They were clerks who trained once a week in hand to hand and then complained how sore they were while dreading the next training session.

Ru smiled, sad, and nodded. "Not for you."

"I don't…" Ale sighed, shook her head sharply as she allowed herself to drop into her own dialect, the one that came easiest to her. "Don' want th' same things, three of us. Don' wanna protect them. Wanna be protected. No more fightin' and killin' and runnin'."

"Fuck do I understand that," Ru groaned. "Makes this harder, though. I got a mission and I think you're the right choice for it."

Ale stared at him. Stared a bit more as Ru whistled and studied the ceiling, kicking that leg draped over the arm of his seat. Then glowered at him as Ru's cheeks started to go red.

"Mission."

"Mmm, yeah," Ru said. His ears started blushing along with his face. "A mission."

"I will stab you," Ale snarled at him.

He grinned, suddenly, shockingly, meeting her eyes. There was laughter there but also wrinkles around his eyes that spoke of stress. Fear. The need of backup.

Which could not, apparently, be given by his mate Nthanda. Or any of the Ceelen. And, given who Ru was, that meant that it had to have something to do with the Hyun-Ju. Seong and Munashe had been gossiping just last night that there was a large contract for shipping munitions that needed to be negotiated between the Hyun-Ju and the Gensyn.

Weapon systems which could handle the Gensyn system's terrible radiation, solar flares and constant waves of shifting debris were very expensive and very hard to manufacture. The Hyun-Ju were the only ones who built manned systems that could handle that environment, specifically in an effort to cajole contracts out of the myriad of independent Gensyn stations.

"My nanites have been upgraded to Gensyn levels," Ale allowed.

"See?" Ru exclaimed, beaming at her as the stress wrinkles around his eyes smoothed out. "That's why I wanna take you. For real, you're super-fast on the uptake, Ale. Got the best scores outta all the Undercity peeps."

"Not a peep," Ale grumbled at him. "Never had a card, couldn't be a peep."

"Pfft, like cards make the peep," Ru said, rolling his eyes as he waved off her very logical and true objections. "Tell you what, lot of those uppers weren't ever gonna be peeps even if you held a gun to their heads. Know that's true 'cause I've done it."

Which sent Ale into snickers because yes, over the last three months she'd seen exactly that. So many idiots among those who lived Above. Hexal City's upper levels, the ones open to the air and sky and infrequent rain that swept over the deserts of Melin, were safe and clean and absolutely filled to the brim with people who couldn't be trusted to know a knife as it cut their throats.

"Mission?" Ale asked, a little less annoyed about being set up this way just because Ru did look truly grateful.

"I gotta go to the Hyun-Ju command ship," Ru said, grimacing. "Can't take Nthanda. He's got a big contract of his own to negotiate with Mellin's new government. Can't take Bala 'cause she's full-consorting with Imani. And Imani's the one keeping Nthanda from cutting throats. Can't take Jing because he's off with Iman doing who knows what and getting shot at. All the people I'd take, they got work. So I looked at the new people. Of them, you're the best, Ale. No joke, best by far. Hardest worker, smartest, fitting in fastest, most adaptable. Also most dangerous and hey, we are talking Hyun-Ju. They respect that."

Ale nodded. True enough though she had a hard time believing that she was that much better than everyone else who'd been evacuated out of the Undercity and given a new life on the Ceelen ships. Five thousand people so far and more joining up every day as Mellin changed into a world where their skills were hunted, hated and outlawed.

President Borna Truman was changing everything with the sort of iron determination that only came from being freed from slavery and being given absolute power.

"What'm I to do?" Ale asked.

"Watch my back," Ru said, ticking points off on his fingers. "Watch them and see what they're up to. I know they're up to something. Both sides. The negotiators on both sides are slime given legs."

Ale snorted, one hand over her mouth to hide her grin. Lovely. She'd have to keep her knives very sharp around the negotiators.

"And," Ru said, grimacing apologetically, "like it if you could help me understand the damned contract. You're studying that shit. I'm too busy taking care of babies, Nthanda and learning to rule to pick contacts apart."

"Oh, I can do that," Ale said. What a relief. Something that wasn't watching for death constantly. "Sure. We taking guards, I hope?"

"Like I'd go anywhere without them anymore," Ru said so wryly that she snorted and poked the sole of his boot. He grinned. Shrugged and then nodded. "We'll have a bunch. You're going to be my assistant, all official like. Dress however you like. The blacks look good on you. Can keep right on with that if you want."

"I will then," Ale said as she smoothed her hands over her thighs. The armored leather jumpsuit covered with a sleek tunic wasn't what most wore on the *Graceful Swan* but it made Ale comfortable and no one had objected so far. "When do we leave?"

"Tomorrow," Ru said with such a heart-broken sigh that Ale started laughing at him.

Ridiculous boy.

This might be better than Ale had expected. A good job, either way. She settled in to negotiate her wages. No reason to be foolish. Having good pay for this was just as important as anything else.

After all, who knew how long Ale would keep her place on the *Graceful Swan*? A person like her wasn't likely to stay forever. Having money to support herself as she found a new home would be important.

2. QUIET TONGUES

THE SHUTTLE ECHOED WITH SILENCE. Eka bit xyr lip and did xyr best to not squirm. Not twitch. Not sigh and crane xyr neck at the other people in the shuttle. Xe didn't succeed very well at that because xe only managed about thirty seconds of stillness before xe absolutely had to move.

What. The. Hell?

This entire expedition was making xem twitch. Eka had never minded leaving the Gensyn system. Not having to know where ever shelter within a quick run was would always be nice. Having some surety that the station wasn't going to blow up randomly or get meteorites punching through the hull was a relief. And, frankly, getting away from xyr family was a good thing. There were only so many lectures and worried questions about Eka's future romances than xe could handle without snapping. That was why xe had been perfectly happy to go off with Dominique when xe suggested that they'd make a good team.

Because while Dominique Goldhirsch was rich and ran three companies at the same time, xe wasn't any good at evaluating weapon system designs. Xyr family was way rich, way powerful, way good at organizing pretty much everything one could think of but weapons design wasn't one of their specialties. Testing them once they were done? Oh, sure. Dominique was stellar at that. Just not making sure that the design met the agreed upon specs.

That was Eka's specialty. Xe'd devoted most of xyr life to designing weapon systems that could blow even the smallest asteroids out of space before they could hit a station. Or, you now, take out an attacking ship. Given the way the Gensyn stations quarreled, it happened with fair regularity despite the hazards of their solar system.

Ma always said that it was a sad, sad thing that the galaxy had fallen so far that even the Gensyn needed to worry about pirates but honestly, it'd been that way since long before Ma was born. Grandma couldn't remember the Drath coming through. She'd been too young to remember it. This was just the way the galaxy was.

Though.

Yeah.

More and more systems were being found every day with lost human colonies. Made sense that the criminals on those worlds would flee up into space looking for an easy credit. Too bad for them that the galaxy was already full of people exploiting all the good niches already. So what else was there to do but turn to crime, right?

Yeah. Right. People always took the easy way out, no matter how much trouble it caused everyone else. Human nature was the one thing that no colony of humanity had ever managed to change. Humans were humans were humans and that was just how it was.

Even cold as ice Dominque was a human when it came down to it. Xe rarely showed xyr emotions, true, but xe bled when stabbed and screamed when infuriated. Still wasn't sure how Dominque and Brogan had met, much less fallen in love, but they had and they seemed happy together.

Most of the time. Right now, Dominque seemed okay but Brogan's normal confident smile and rambling dialog about everything under the sun had transformed into twitches and silence. So damned weird. Eka hadn't ever seen Brogan this quiet the entire time xe'd known xem. Years now. Made xyr skin crawl to have bluff, cheerful Brogan acting like xe was terrified. Or at least worried sick about something. Especially with Dominique showing no signs of strain at all.

Eka peeked at Dominique again.

Nope, still reading so calmly that xe might have not even noticed that the cabin was dead-silent. How the hell did Dominique do that? Eka had never figured that one out. Must be a Goldhirsch thing, special training along with how to handle money, be diplomatic with people that you want to shoot on sight and reading financial charts like Eka could read a wiring diagram.

"Two minutes," Brogan said up at the stick.

"Good," Dominique said. Xe glanced at Eka and winked as xe turned xyr pad off.

Eka blushed, cursing at xemself for being an idiot. Mostly. What were Dominique and Brogan arguing about? Had to be some sort of argument. They were normally so chatty that Eka wanted to stuff something in xyr mouths just to get a little peace. This quiet was freaking xyr out.

But then this whole deal was weird from the outset. Making an alliance with the Hyun-Ju? Sure, sure, that made sense. They were the best shipping and manufacturing family around, at least for the sorts of things that Dominique would be handling for this deal. Weapons, armor plating, sensors for weapon systems, plus skeletons for new ships. Not people-moving ships but attack ships. You wanted to move people, that was the Ceelen.

What bugged Eka, what xe hadn't managed to convey to either Dominique or Brogan, was that this whole thing smelled off.

They didn't need ship killer weapons. The Gensyn system flatly wasn't one that'd allow those weapons to work properly over the distance needed for a ship-to-ship battle. Too much debris and way too much radiation screwing with everything. Sheer amount of coronal ejections going through would fry beams before they got to another ship and frankly? Eka still couldn't design a weapon that would deliver a solid projectile on a straight trajectory for more than one light second.

Outside the Gensyn?

Sure, they'd be useful as all hell. You could take out any ship you crossed paths with, Ceelen super-liner to Old Earth Dreadnought, not that Old Earth's dreadnoughts were really the peak of technology.

More like cast-backs to the old generation ships that'd carried humanity to the stars with FTL engines slapped on them.

"You're quiet," Dominique commented as Brogan maneuvered them into the indicated landing bay on the Hyun-Ju flagship.

"Me?" Eka said, staring at xem. "You're the ones silent as space without a suit."

Brogan only snorted. Kept xyr eyes firmly locked on the displays even though they were on automated landing sequence. Dominique only shrugged and damn it all, what was going on with them? Couldn't be their relationship falling apart. They'd been joined hip and tit since they were tiny. Eka huffed.

"Fine, don't tell me," Eka grumbled. "Leave me hanging without a damn lifeline."

Xe focused inwards on the nanite trigger that allowed xyr to shift from apparently female to more masculine appearance. It didn't make too many changes to xyr appearance. Smaller tits, slightly less ass and a bit more obvious package in front. Xe wasn't one of the really obvious shifters that sprouted tits the size of xyr head but hey, Eka always felt stronger in masculine form.

And it drove Dominique nuts.

"I thought I asked you to stay feminine," Dominique snapped at Eka. First real emotion xe'd shown since this whole deal came up.

Eka glowered at xem. "Don't you dare tell me how to present, Dominique. We're friends. Not lovers. Nor married. You're not even my employer. I'm doing this strictly as a favor. You try and pull that crap on me and I'm not only gone, I'll go to their side and tell them all the things you don't want them to know about what you need."

Dominique's eyes went wide. Brogan's head snapped around, xyr mouth open as if to protest. Xe swallowed hard and then started so hard that xe nearly fell out of xyr seat when the landing bay clamped onto their shuttle and set them down.

Oh yeah, they were definitely up to something.

Problem was that Eka still didn't know what. Suspicions weren't proof. And xe'd need proof if xe was going to get anyone to listen to xem. Worse problem was that Eka was pretty much on xyr own if Dominque and Brogan weren't going to back xyr up.

"You wouldn't dare," Dominique whispered as xe stood, pad clutched so tight that xyr knuckles were white.

"Push me and you'll find out," Eka snapped at xyr. "I'm not yours. Don't try to claim me or control me. And don't you ever tell me what to present as again. My body is mine and I'm not sharing it with either of you. Right now, you're damned lucky to get me to share my mind far enough to look at those plans."

Brogan bit xyr lip as xe stood, waving both of them out of the cabin. "Let's not argue right now, please? Yes, there's more going on. Just... give us a bit of slack to get the work done, will you?"

Eka snorted. "I'll give you slack. For now. But you keep this up I'll cut the line and leave you drifting. I'm not your tool, Brogan. I thought I was your friend. I stood for both of you at your wedding. I've supported you through everything so far. This sudden lack of information is about to make me crawl out of my skin and you will not like what happens if you keep it up."

Both Brogan and Dominique flinched at the mention of the wedding. It'd been a bit more than standing for them. Brogan's family had tried to raid the wedding, tried to kidnap xem away from Dominique's side because xe'd flatly refused to fund their gambling and slaving enterprises. Eka had fought for them, bled for them, killed for them. Made the hurt of being untrusted all the more painful.

Made the fear that xe'd been a fool and a patsy all this time that much worse, too.

"It's not something we can discuss here," Dominique said, waving towards the ship around them. The Hyun-Ju waiting outside.

"All the more reason you shoulda been talking hard and fast on our way here," Eka snapped. "Let's go. I want this done so we can head back and you can do that talking. One way or the other, I'm not going to play shield for you guys if you won't be honest with me."

"We will," Brogan said so earnestly that Eka almost trusted xem. Almost. Xyr eyes shifted away from Eka's, away from Dominique. Licked xyr lips and xyr breath caught like xyr heart had started pounding.

Eka stared at xem until xe flushed. Looked at Dominique but xe had that perfect mask of genteel control and politeness on xyr face.

Nothing to see there. Except that xe'd never once used that face on Eka. Not once.

"Go," Eka snapped at Dominique. "Let's get it over with."

They went first, Dominique at the head, Brogan right behind xem. Eka trailed a couple of paces behind. Watching them. Yeah, they were up to something. Brogan had a bunch more weapons tucked into xyr clothes than normal. Not to mention that xe was solidly male right now and Dominique hated that. But Brogan was one of the ones who shifted hard to male. Right now you'd think that xe was about to grow a beard that bushed out about a foot and lift things three times xyr weight.

Eka hadn't noticed during boarding but Dominique had put on heeled shoes. Actual three-inch heels that made xyr hips sway enticingly. And xe'd worn a tunic long enough to come down and hide xyr groin from prying eyes. Xe looked very, very female right now. Perfectly groomed hair, feminine clothes, touch of makeup on xyr eyes and lips.

As xe walked, Eka focused and shifted to pure neutral. Not male, not female, as androgynous as only a shifting Gensyn could be. Let them look 'normal' to the Hyun-Ju. Eka was Gensyn and be damned if xe'd let anyone forget it.

All of which disappeared from Eka's mind as xe stepped off the shuttle ramp and out into the landing bay. Who the hell designed this thing? The open space was impressive for the engineering of the space but that was so much air. Could they really afford to lose that much air if there was a breach? Pure idiocy to have it this huge. The stupid landing bay was easily a thousand yards long and wide, about half that high, filled with cranes and hanging cradles full of fighters waiting to be called upon.

Good launching tube would be better than those cradles.

"Focus, Eka," Dominique murmured as the Hyun-Ju party approached. Xyr lips were too tight when xe saw that Eka had shifted again.

"Fine," Eka murmured right back. "You do the same."

Dominique's profession smile slapped into place. Good. Let xyr focus on the Hyun-Ju. Eka would keep right on working on figuring out what was going on.

Or at least that was what xe intended to do.

All xyr plans and irritation disappeared when Eka actually focused on the people coming to meet them. There were Hyun-Ju with their narrow faces and long hair in sleek black falls on their back. Good dozen of them, all armed with blasters and swords. Like anyone had sword battles in this day and age.

But in the front of them was a short woman with a round broad face, dressed all in black. She had hair cut so short that Eka could see her scalp. Small bust, muscular arms, thighs to crush your skull. And narrowed eyes that swept over Dominique's so-proper smile with nothing but scorn.

"I am Ale Aukema, assistant to King Ru Sashi," she said. Held herself like a warrior about to rip them to little shreds. Damn. "You will follow me."

"Thank you for having us," Dominique started to say only to falter as Ale glowered at xyr. What a glower, too, complete with curled lip, raised chin and a little snort of pure annoyance that made Eka want to crow with delight.

"You will follow me," Ale said so coldly that Eka couldn't help but grin at her. "King Ru is waiting. Pleasantries can wait until you meet him."

"Ah, of course," Dominique said. Xe cleared xyr throat. "We look forward to seeing him."

Ale nodded, swept her eyes over Brogan so dismissively that xe flinched before raising an eyebrow at Eka. Oh, what a wonder Ale was! Eka laughed and bowed just as extravagantly as xe could because how could xe not?

"Looking forward to working with you," Eka said, grinning at the sheer disgust in Ale's eyes. "I hope I get to see you tear someone apart. It'd be a thing of wonder."

The disgust transformed into shock and then amusement. Ale raised her chin, smirking at Eka with so much confidence that both Brogan and Dominique glowered at Eka for flirting.

"You're not that important that I would demonstrate for your pleasure," Ale said but she smirked as she said it and there was a little blush over her round cheeks.

"Nope," Eka said, laughing. "Don't care. I'd still love to see you in action. Nothing better than a vicious warrior taking down everything."

"I don't know," Ale said, turning away. She strode away from them, the Hyun-Ju warriors parting for her without the slightest change of expression. "I always thought that having someone trusted at your back was better."

She looked over her shoulder, speared Dominique and Brogan with that look and then raised an eyebrow at Eka.

"Oh, I'm in love," Eka breathed because yes. So much yes. To see it that fast? And just show it right off? "Lead on, Ale Aukema. I'm eager to see what you've got for us."

Ale didn't change her stride in the slightest. "Then keep up. I don't wait for anyone."

Dominique tried to hiss something at Eka but xe was already moving. This sure wasn't what xe'd expected on this trip. It was way, way better. Even if Eka did have to betray Dominique and Brogan, Eka would be happy about it having gotten to meet Ale. What a wonder, Ale Aukema, assistant and killer and brilliant woman that Eka would almost leave the Gensyn system for even though they'd only just met.

OTHER DRATH BOOKS BY MEYARI MCFARLAND:

Clash of Lines
Joining of Lines
Consort of the Crystal Palace
Fragments of a Chain
Stranded With You
Reunited Hearts
A Simple Life
Cradle of the Day

Also Available: The collected Drath Series:
The Drath Series Books 1-3
The Drath Series Books 4-6

You can find these and many other books at www.MDR-Publishing.com. Please sign up for our mailing list to get regular updates on the latest preorders and new releases and a free ebook!

AFTERWORD

The Drath series is one part of a very large, very epic, multi-thousand years long story in my head. There's bits and pieces all through time and space, on earth, in orbit and on many, many other planets. There's a good thirty thousand years or so worth of history to it that's been percolating in my head for literal decades.

Thankfully, it's a story that's relatively easy to break into chunks. Even smaller ones like the previous novels in the series. The more far-flung bits of the story are different series entirely, which is fine. Someday I'll put out a timeline and a map of sorts that says how all of it connects.

Not yet, though.

There's too much left to write in the other pieces.

That said, I'm deeply pleased to get this book out. With this book, the Drath series shifts away from the Romance / Space Opera focus and goes at high speed into Space Opera / Adventure with found family tropes. There's been a war brewing behind the scenes in all the previous novels. Also in many of the short stories that I should collect properly someday.

This is the opening salvo of an alien galactic war that's going to change everything for the Drath, for Humanity, and for the rest of the galaxy to boot. I've been dying to get it started and I'm looking forward to getting the next book out soon-ish, too.

I'm with Narcisse on leaping right into the battle. At least I won't be dodging blaster bolts and telepathic squid-aliens. Looking forward to taking you on the next step of the ride!

If you want more stories like this one, please go sign up for my newsletter on www.MDR-Publishing.com. You'll get updates on whatever I've got coming up, special deals and you can get a free ebook or collection of my short stories. Or you can sign up at my Patreon and get access to my art, writing and whatever's going on creatively in my life.

Thank you for reading!

Meyari McFarland

April, 2024

www.MDR-Publishing.com

AUTHOR BIO

MEYARI MCFARLAND HAS BEEN TELLING stories since she was a small child. Her stories range from adventures appropriate to children to erotica but they always feature strong characters who do what they think is right no matter what gets in their way.

Meyari has been married for twenty years and has no children or pets. She lives in the Puget Sound, WA and enjoys the fog, rain and cool weather that are typical here. When vacation times come, she and her husband usually go somewhere warm like Hawaii or they go on their own adventures to Japan and other far away countries.

Her life has included jobs ranging from cleaning motel rooms, food service, receptionist, building and editing digital maps, auditing and document control.

MORE FROM MEYARI MCFARLAND

Website:

www.MDR-Publishing.com

SOCIAL MEDIA:

Patreon - https://www.patreon.com/meyarimcfarland
Mastodon – https://wandering.shop/@MeyariMcFarland
Pillowfort - https://www.pillowfort.social/Meyari
Facebook - https://www.facebook.com/meyari.mcfarland.5
Pinterest - https://www.pinterest.com/meyarim/

If you enjoyed this story, please leave a comment on your favorite site. Also, please sign up for the newsletter so that you can hear about the latest preorders and new releases.

Printed in the USA
CPSIA information can be obtained
at www.ICGtesting.com
LVHW091912240424
778354LV00023B/89/J

9 781643 092119